5: ANDY THE PRISONER

"Can I have a telephone number where I can contact you, Mum?" I asked her in the middle of the packing.

"We'll be travelling around quite a bit at first … but as soon as we can we'll give you a number. Until then, we'll phone you."

Something funny was going on and I was determined to find out what. I was also getting ideas flashing through my mind about how to go to the café without Grandma Sorrell being any wiser. I tried to shake these thoughts away before they were able to take root in my brain, and start growing into full-scale plans. Because once I get an idea that only needs courage to carry out, I have to do it. Something makes me. That's how I got my name – the daring one.

The CAFÉ Club

5: ANDY THE PRISONER

Ann Bryant

Hippo

For Little Granny

Scholastic Children's Books,
Commonwealth House, 1–19 New Oxford Street,
London WC1A 1NU, UK
a division of Scholastic Ltd
London ~ New York ~ Toronto ~ Sydney ~ Auckland

First published by Scholastic Ltd, 1996

Copyright © Ann Bryant, 1996

ISBN 0 590 13653 4

Typeset by TW Typesetting, Midsomer Norton, Avon

Printed by Cox & Wyman Ltd, Reading, Berks.

All rights reserved

10 9 8 7 6 5 4 3 2 1

The right of Ann Bryant to be identified as the author
of this work has been asserted by her in accordance with the
Copyright, Designs and Patents Act, 1988.

Chapter 1

Hi! I'm Andy.

My real name's Agnès, which you pronounce Ann-yes. You see, my mum is French and my dad is English so that makes me half French. All my friends call me Andy, though.

I've got five main friends, we're all thirteen and we all go to Cableden Comp. There's one other thing that we all do too, and that's take it in turns to work at a café in Cableden. If it's an after school day we do two hours and if it's a Saturday we get to do four. It all works on a rota basis.

Let me tell you about my friends. I'll start with my best friend, Leah Bryan. She's the musician. She's really talented at playing the violin and the piano. She's dedicated to her music and I really admire that kind of determination and persistence, especially as so many kids of our age think it's really "sad" to learn a musical instrument.

1

Leah's got long pale hair and a very calm face. She also gets first prize for being the biggest worrier in our group.

Fen is short for Fenella Brooks, the ambitious one. We wouldn't all be working at the café if it hadn't been for Fen hassling her aunt Jan to let us. Jan is the manageress of the café. She's firm but fair with the six of us. Fen is thin and strong and very tomboyish. She's got light brown hair nearly to her shoulders.

Fen's best friend is Tash. She's very dark with quite short thick hair and bright eyes. Her full name is Natasha Johnston and we call her the peacemaker – calm and sensible all the time.

Then there's Luce, or Lucy Edmunson, the crazy one. Luce's hair is a wild mass of strawberry-blonde curls, and her life is a wild mass of events. People say that trouble seeks Luce out, but Luce just laughs at that.

Her best friend is Jaimini Riva, the brainy one. Jaimini and Luce are like chalk and cheese in looks and character. With a black father and a white mother, Jaimini came out a beautiful coffee colour. She's got long shiny black hair and big dark eyes. Oh, and you pronounce Jaimini, Jay-m-nee, by the way.

I suppose her colouring is the nearest of all to mine. My skin is what they call olive, and my eyes and hair are dark brown. The difference is that my hair is very short indeed. I like it like that because I'm not all that interested in spending ages on make-up or hair. I'm into sport and gym, and everybody thinks I'm also into adventure, but I'm not really.

They call me the daring one and they think I'm really brave, but it's not that. It's just that I kind of make myself do things. I can't help it. If I get an idea about something I can't leave it alone. In a way I'm as mad as Luce but the difference is that Luce doesn't think about things, she just does them, whereas I think every time.

My mum worries about me. She's certain I'm going to land myself in great danger. Mum says that Dad worries about me too, and that that's why he's so strict about letting me do things. She says he's only trying to protect me, but I'm not so sure about that.

I've told you that I'm supposed to be the daring one and the others think nothing scares me. Well, there is one thing that scares me, and that's my dad. I once heard someone describe him as a hard, cold man. I wasn't supposed to hear that but I did, and I think about it often. I told Mum that I'd heard and she said I shouldn't take any notice because underneath he's really soft-hearted. Most of the time I can't believe that, but just once or twice Dad's surprised me when his defences have come down and he's shown himself as a proud, loving father. I wish I could see that side of him more often, I really do.

Tash lives with her mum and doesn't see her dad any more, but that's made her really close to her mum. Luce has got a stepdad and she seems to be even closer to him than she is to her real dad. The other three are all closer to their mums than to their dads, except perhaps Leah, who's got a sweet, old-fashioned father. I envy them all because it's just not quite the same in my family. I've got a little brother, Sebastien, aged thirteen months, who comes in for a lot of gooey attention. The attention that *I* get seems to involve telling me things I'm not allowed to do, or otherwise things I should be doing more of, like homework.

Dad works in France which is where Mum and Dad met. The first time they ever came over to visit England, Mum fell in love with it, and after a few more visits she said she wanted to settle here. My grandmother lives about six miles away from us. That's my dad's mother. Her husband, my grandpa, died quite a few years ago.

My grandparents on Mum's side live in France so I don't see them much. I sometimes wish it was the other way round because my French grandparents are absolutely lovely, full of fun and affection. The French in general do a lot more kissing than the English, but Mami and Papi (as all French children call their grandparents), really take the biscuit for doing the most kissing. Sometimes they give me three on each cheek. I wish they lived in England near us, then I could see them every day. My biggest fear is that they'll fall ill and we'll be too far away to look after them.

I was thinking about my grandmother on Dad's side as I was going into work. I'd already sprinted to the café from school and carried on running for another ten minutes, then turned and walked back. I'd just had double maths, you see, and my body feels like it wants to explode when I've been sitting still for one hour forty minutes, so that's why I decided to get rid of some energy before starting work at the café. You never know from one week to the next whether or not you'll be lucky enough to be buzzing round clearing tables, serving drinks etc.

I went through the back door into the kitchen and was greeted by Kevin, who is the chef and also one of my best mates. I know that's a strange thing to say about a guy of twenty-one, but I get on really well with Kevin. Luce fancies him (because apparently he's really good-looking, so she keeps telling me), but the others just look on him as a joker because he's always in a good mood and often cracks jokes which he thinks are about a hundred times funnier than they really are.

There's a very kind side to Kevin too, but I reckon the reason I like him so much is because he's very fit and keen on working out at the gym, and because he's a man of very few words. He never makes small talk unless he's being funny and not really concentrating. I guess a lot must go on in that brain of his while he's cooking away! Jan says he's an expert chef and she dreads him leaving the café. I'm with Jan on that.

"Hiya, Squidge," he said as I shut the door behind me. He doesn't usually smile at people much, Kevin doesn't. He just smiles to himself, but on this occasion he actually honoured me with a grin. I don't mind him calling me Squidge. I wouldn't like it coming from anyone else but I don't mind from Kevin. After all, it's true that I'm easily the smallest in our group of friends.

"Hiya, Kev. What's cooking?" He ignored my question. Typical!

"Look at this – good for the thigh muscles."

A good deal of our conversation tends to be on physical fitness and I was curious to see whatever it was Kevin was about to demonstrate. I watched, puzzled, as he heaved a heavy, free-standing cupboard away from the wall, so that the back of it was about forty centimetres from the sink; he then leaned against it, bent his knees so he looked as though he was sitting in an imaginary chair and pretended he was washing up. I didn't say any-thing, just waited till he'd moved away to let me have a go, then tried it out. I immediately felt the pull in my thigh muscles, but when I reached out to the sink my arms weren't long enough.

"Not one of your best ideas, Kev," I told him, as he pretended to head-butt the cupboard, as though it was *its* fault! This is the scene that Jan came into from the café.

"Stop making a gymnasium out of my kitchen," she said to Kevin in mock temper. "I'll have that cupboard back in its place, please. Hello, Andy. Good day at school?"

"Apart from double maths," I told her.

"Quite good then," she said with a smile.

"And double English," I added.

"Not very good then," she said as the smile faded and an absent-minded look took its place.

"And history and RE," I finished off.

"The pits," Kevin concluded, brushing his hands off as though moving the heavy cupboard back was no more of a feat than flouring a pastry board. I put one of the white aprons on top of my black school skirt, rolled up my sleeves and set to, washing up an enormous pile of cooking utensils and pots and pans.

"Dee's in there, Andy," Jan said as she made her way back into the café from the kitchen. "When you've finished the washing-up she wants a quick word with you."

"What's it about?"

Too late. The door swung to, leaving me

wondering why Fen's mother, Dee, who is also Jan's sister, wanted a word with me. I glanced over at Kevin and decided not to even bother asking him if he knew why. He wasn't interested in anything social so he wouldn't have taken it in, even if Jan *had* told him why Dee wanted to speak to me.

As the pile of washing-up slowly went down my thoughts got back to Grandma Sorrell – Dad's mum. I wanted to call her Gran or Granny but she was most insistent that it had to be Grandma Sorrell and nothing else. She's strict and bossy, very independent, rather snobby and extremely intolerant of everything. Her husband, my grandpa, on the other hand, was a really lovely man. I don't often cry but I cried buckets when he died.

Grandma Sorrell belongs in a Charles Dickens book, really. She's tall and thin with glasses and a walking stick, and she smells of something like a cross between disinfectant and the most awful musky perfume. She hardly ever smiles, but on the few occasions she does, her cheeks form loads of little cracky lines and her mouth turns up only the teeniest bit as though it didn't really want to, but the cheeks gave it no choice. Her eyes don't come into it at all.

Leah met Grandma Sorrell once and afterwards I asked her what she thought of the old dragon, and Leah replied, "Oh, she's not that bad really, Andy…"

"Tell me one nice thing about her then," I challenged.

"Well, she's got nice…"

"Yes?"

"She's got nice … furniture."

After Leah had said that there was a long pause while we both thought about it, then at exactly the same moment we cracked up laughing and proceeded to have a ridiculous conversation where I pretended to be Grandma Sorrell and Leah pretended to be a gentleman admirer.

"Oh, Mrs Sorrell," Leah had said, falling to her knees and clutching her heart dramatically, "I just love your mahogany chest."

"Don't be cheeky, you nasty little man," I'd retorted in my primmest, poshest voice, then we had both fallen about laughing again.

"What are you grinning at?" Becky asked me as she plonked a pile of plates next to the dishwasher.

"Oh, nothing," I told her because I couldn't be bothered to explain and anyway it wouldn't be funny second-hand. Becky rolled her eyes and pulled open the dishwasher door.

Either Mark or Becky is always on duty with one of us lot. They're both really nice but I especially like Mark because he's training in the martial arts which is very disciplined physically, and Mark is my kind of person. He only left school last year so he's not all that much older than me. Becky's a bit older than that and she's a very down to earth character who's worked with Jan for ages. The other person who works at the café is Debra, but we don't see her so much because she works from nine till three so she's gone before we get there.

"Dee Brooks wants a quick word with you when you're not too busy," Becky told me. I'd more or less finished the washing-up so I went through to the café and glanced round to look for Dee. She was sitting with Rachel, Fen's nine-year-old sister, and Emmy, their five-year-old sister, and a girl I hadn't ever seen before. She looked about five, too. She also looked as though she was about to burst into tears.

Dee's face lit up when she saw me. "Oh, Andy, sorry to interrupt you, pet…" Fen's mum, Dee, was very much like her sister Jan. For one thing they both said "pet". "This little girl," she went on, indicating the worried-looking child seated beside Emmy, "is new at Rachel and Emmy's school. She's called Marine and she's bilingual. She speaks fluent French and English like you. I met her mum outside school and offered to bring Marine to the café with Rachel and Emmy." Dee lowered her voice and leaned towards me so Marine wouldn't hear what she was about to say.

"Apparently she's not joining in with anything

at school and the teacher says she hasn't uttered a single word since she's been there. Some sort of problem at home, I gather. I just wondered whether or not it might help Marine to have someone outside of her family to talk French to her."

"Comment t'appelles-tu?" I began, turning to the little girl with a bright smile. The teeniest flicker of understanding appeared for a second on her face, but she didn't answer me.

"And you're sure she speaks French?" I checked with Dee in a whisper.

"Quite sure."

"Quel âge as-tu?" I tried again.

"She's seven," Emmy answered.

"Oh, that was clever of you, Emmy. I didn't know you could speak French." I smiled at Fen's younger sister.

"I understand those two things what you just said," Emmy answered, "'cos everyone starts by asking her that."

"Oh, sorry to be so boring," I joked with Emmy, then I turned back to Marine. *"Tu as sept ans?"* I asked her, because I wanted to check she was seven. She certainly didn't look it.

Again her eyes narrowed very slightly but she offered no answer. I decided that perhaps if I spoke rapidly in a mixture of French and English it might kind of shock her into reacting. So looking directly into her eyes I gabbled on about how difficult it was at first in a strange new place, and how I knew how she must feel, but not to worry because soon she'd start to like her school and she'd find some good friends. Then I asked her if she had any pets. Getting no response to that I asked her if Mummy was at home and what she was doing – anything to try to get her to speak.

It was no good. Marine's eyes had glazed over and she wasn't even looking at me any more. I may as well have been speaking double Dutch.

"We'd better be going," Dee said with a sigh as she handed me a ten-pound note. I shrugged and said I was sorry. "Thanks for trying anyway, pet."

I took the bill for table seven off the number board at the counter, rang up the items and gave Dee back her change before returning to the kitchen. On a sudden impulse I turned at the kitchen door to watch the little party leave the café. Rachel and Emmy had gone on ahead and Dee was pushing open the door with Marine standing just behind her. I was on the point of disappearing into the kitchen when she turned round and gave me a little wave. I waved back and mouthed *"Salut"* across the café. There was no response to my goodbye but I felt that at least I'd achieved something, however minuscule.

I must have been frowning as I walked over to

the sink because Jan shot me a quick concerned glance. "All right, Andy?"

I nodded and started drying the stuff on the draining board.

"Do it with your arms out straight," Kevin said casually. "Good for the deltoid muscles."

I tried for about five seconds but it was another non-starter. "I'll stick to training outside of work hours," I told him with a grin.

The moment I walked through the door of our house that evening I sensed an atmosphere. Dad was away. I knew that, yet it was almost as though he'd come home again. The house somehow feels different when he's around. My little brother Sebastien came tottering up to meet me. Well, he almost met me but he's not very good at walking without holding on to things he fell back on to his padded bottom a few times.

Our house is big, in fact it's bigger than any of my close friends' houses. I know Leah and the others are impressed by it, but I'm not. I'd really rather live in a cosier place. I love going to Leah's house and I'm very flattered because her dad really likes me, apparently. I like him, too. He's so nice and quiet and just sits there puffing on his pipe. I sometimes play chess or draughts with him if Leah has to do some practice or something.

Mum appeared behind Sebastien. Her hands

were clasped together, which was a sure sign that she had something to tell me, and I knew instinctively that I wasn't going to like it. I looked at her with her high-heeled black and gold shoes, her shiny tights and her lovely pale green suit with a black body underneath. Her short dark hair was, as usual, immaculate and her gold earrings made her tiny face look even more striking. There's no doubt about it, my mother is beautiful.

My friends almost gasp when they see her. Fen is probably the least impressed because she doesn't notice people's looks as much as the others. Mum speaks English with a strong French accent. That's the other thing that the English find attractive about her. I wish I was closer to her. I mean it's not that we get on badly – we don't. In fact, we rarely argue. It's just that Mum worships the ground that Dad walks on, even though I think she's a little scared of him herself. And of course, Sebastien, being tiny, needs a lot of her attention. So sometimes I get the feeling I'm the least important person in our family.

"I have someseeng to tell you, *bibiche*." She always called me "*bibiche*". It's a term of endearment in French. I waited.

"You faazer telephoned and he has an important business treep in Sardeenia…"

My heart beat a little bit faster as I thought, Yes, get to the point Mum.

"He wants me to go weez heem."

Still I waited while an awful possibility surfaced in my brain. "Does this mean Sebastien and I are coming too?" I wondered.

"Sebastien weel stay weez Mami and Papi…"

"In France?"

"Yes."

"And me?" Surely she wasn't going to let me stay here on my own. I began to feel excited.

"But you cannot stay at Mami's because of your school."

I nodded.

"So we have decided zat eet ees best for you to stay weez *Grand-mère* Sorrell."

"What!!"

It was her turn to wait now. I felt gutted. Gutted and cross. It was all right saying "*We* have decided," but I knew exactly who had made that decision – my father. It irritated me that even though I'm thirteen I don't get included in their plans. I just get told when it's all been arranged. At least I presumed it had all been arranged. How weird, I thought, that I should have only been thinking about Grandma Sorrell that day.

"I'm not staying with her. She creaks when she walks," I said rather childishly. Mum couldn't help smiling. She unclasped her hands and put

15

her arm round my shoulders, but only for a second because we both suddenly realized that Sébastien was out of sight and very quiet indeed, which usually meant trouble.

"Sebastien, petit coquin, où es-tu?" Mum called in the voice she kept especially for him. She hurried into the kitchen and I followed her. He wasn't there.

"I'll try the playroom," I said. We both knew he wouldn't be upstairs because the gate at the bottom of the staircase was firmly shut. I could hear Mum's voice coming from the lounge, all soft and loving as she spoke in French, pretending to be cross. I felt a little stab of jealousy, sharply followed by a severe voice in my head telling me to stop being so pathetic. After all, I was lucky to have a little brother. Jaimini would give anything to have a brother or sister. She's an only child, you see, but her mum's pregnant so she won't have long to wait for her wish to come true.

Mum reappeared with Sebastien in her arms. "He was examining zee contents of zee waste paper basket," she told me with an affectionate smile as she rubbed noses with Sebastien, making him giggle. The little break in our conversation didn't make going back to it any easier.

"Grand-mère Sorrell does not creak," Mum said with an attempt at light-heartedness.

"She does. And she stinks of something resembling moth balls."

"It won't be for long," Mum said, changing tack.

"How many days?"

"We … we don't know exactly…"

"What do you mean? Surely you know how long Dad's business trip is for."

"Not exactly…"

Something told me the worst was yet to come.

"Maybe sree weeks…"

"Three weeks! Oh Mum, no!" She bit her lip and put Sebastien down. "There's no way I'm staying with that stropbag," I continued in one of my rare moments of voicing anger. "She may be my grandmother but she doesn't feel like one."

Mum didn't say anything else as I turned to go up to my room. She knows when I'm really angry. I hardly ever shout, in fact I go quieter if anything. She wouldn't press me for a while. She'd let me get used to the idea. I changed into cycling shorts, T-shirt and trainers.

"I'm going for a run."

"How long will you be?"

"An hour."

With that I left the house and ran all the way across the common and didn't stop till I arrived at Leah's door, where I took my pulse.

"Hi, Andy."

It was Kim who answered the door, Leah's fifteen-year-old sister. She looks very much like Leah but with darker, thicker hair. I like the way she doesn't wear make-up and isn't particularly bothered about fashion, but looks better than all the rest of her friends who are dolled up to the eyeballs.

"Hi, Kim. Is Leah around?"

"She's in her room. Go on up."

"Is she practising?"

"She was, yeah. But don't worry, she'd like an excuse to stop, I bet." When Kim smiles her face completely changes. I've seen boys practically keel over at the sight of her smile. It's amazing.

"Hello, young lady."

That was Leah's dad, Stuart. He's very old-fashioned and sweet. As usual he was puffing on his pipe. Impulsively I gave him a quick kiss.

"Ooh, I'm a lucky chap," he chuckled.

I grinned at him. "Sorry if it was a bit sweaty," I called over my shoulder as I went up to find Leah. I waited outside her door until there was a pause in her violin playing, then pressed my mouth against the door.

"Hi, Leah, it's me."

The door was flung open and a very surprised-looking Leah stood there, her long blonde hair hanging over her violin.

"I'm not disturbing you, am I?"

18

"No, I've finished. Come in. How did it go?"

"What?"

"At the café."

"Oh, fine."

She looked at me carefully.

"Oh dear, something's the matter isn't it? Is it your dad?"

All my friends know that my dad is usually the cause of my problems. I nodded. Leah's face looked so full of concern I felt glad I'd decided to come to her house. I sat on her bed and told her quickly what Mum had just told me.

"We'd come and visit you every day," she said immediately.

"But I can't bear it in her house – and for three weeks too…" I suddenly had a picture of Mum's troubled face. "*We don't know exactly…*"

"There's something funny going on, Leah," I told her in scarcely more than a whisper. "Mum is acting really vague about how long the business trip is. Three weeks was just a figure she plucked out of the air it seemed to me."

"I suppose you can't always tell with business trips. Look on the bright side, perhaps it'll turn out to be only one. I think you ought to question your mum more."

She was right, of course. I'd just done what I always do, gone off for a run to clear my mind and to try and make the situation go away. "Yes, you're right. I'll phone you later if there's anything interesting to report."

I got the history homework off Leah because she's good at history, then gave her a few ideas for the English project, before heading back home.

Mum smiled with relief when she saw me. "What deed Leah have to say?" she asked with a twinkle in her eye.

"How did you know…"

"Because I know my daughter, that's how."

Sebastien had gone to bed so Mum and I sat down to eat at the kitchen table.

"Leah couldn't understand why the business trip doesn't last for an exact length of time," I said, breaking into the dreaded conversation. Mum's eyelashes fluttered. I had touched a nerve, but I couldn't work out what or why.

"Eet may be longer or shorter. You can never tell…"

"You've already said that. Look, what's the big mystery, Mum?"

"No meestery. We just don't know how long eet's going to take this time, that's all."

I sighed. Leah was obviously right. There was nothing more to be said really.

"Zee café…"

"What about it?"

"Your *grand-mère* ees quite old-fashioned and

set in her ways. She weel worry eef you don't come straight home on the bus after school." My eyes must have been smouldering, but Mum had obviously decided to get the whole big bad deal out in the open. "She weel meet you off zee bus every day, and there is no bus after six o'clock, *bibiche*."

"Mum, you must be joking," I said in quiet anger. "I'm not a kid. I won't be treated like one. I'm not giving up the café even for three weeks. I'm part of a team. That's the only way it works."

"Just for a short time…"

"No, Mum. You'll have to tell Dad I refuse to give up the café, that's all. Anyway, if Grandma Sorrell wasn't such a big snob, she'd realize that it's very sensible and grown-up, working in a café."

"It's not because she's a snob that she doesn't want you to work there. Eet's because there's no bus after six and she worries that you're very young to go to work after school."

"Huh!" I answered, more to myself than to Mum. It was a dead-end conversation, because I was sure that even if there had been a bus after six o'clock, Grandma Sorrell wouldn't have let me work in the café.

As I got up from the table a thought entered my head. I would tell Dad myself. I'd make myself do it even though I dreaded the thought.

I went over to the phone and tapped in Dad's French number. After ten rings I replaced the phone.

"No reply," I told Mum unnecessarily. "I'm going to do my homework. I'll try him later."

"He won't change hees mind, you know."

"And I won't change mine," I retorted quietly.

Chapter 2

The next day at morning break the six of us gathered down at the netball courts. We always go down there when we want privacy. I had just finished telling the others my horrible predicament.

"You'll go totally bonkers cloistered up with that old crone," was Luce's not exactly bright prediction.

"Surely if you promised to telephone from the café to reassure her you were safe, then you could catch a later bus," Tash suggested sensibly.

"Apparently there isn't a bus after six," I told her quietly.

"You could always run back to your grand-mother's place, Andy. It'd be great for your training." That was Fen, thinking positively as always. The clouds in my mind passed over for a moment when she said that, but they soon came back when I thought of all the other days of the week.

"I can't bear the idea of never seeing you lot in the café for a Coke when I'm not actually on duty," I told them, feeling helpless all of a sudden. The café was a big part of our lives and we often popped in there, even when it wasn't our turn to work, especially on Saturday afternoons when there was a really good atmosphere.

"I've got it!" Leah suddenly declared. She then put her hands on my shoulders and looked into my eyes as though she was about to tell me that she'd discovered the cure for the common cold. "You must stay at *my* house!"

There was a long pause while the others were presumably doing what I was doing, which was checking there weren't any flaws in Leah's brilliant suggestion, before daring to react to it. Finally, of course, it was Luce who spoke first.

"You are so stunningly clever, young Leah!" she announced, which made us all smile. "Not just a pretty musician, are you?" she added, which caused a few giggles.

"Wouldn't your parents mind?" I asked cautiously.

"Mum and Dad both think you're absolutely wonderful," Leah replied.

"But is there enough room for me?" I went on, trying not to get my hopes up too soon.

24

"Are you kidding? A little squirt like you could kip on the hearth rug!" Luce bubbled on.

"You could sleep on the floor in my room. We've got plenty of sleeping bags," Leah told me.

"What about your grandmother?" Tash asked.

"What about your *dad*?" Jaimini asked. She had a strict dad too, so it was no wonder that problems with fathers would spring quickly to her mind.

"I'm going to phone him tonight," I told them unwaveringly.

"Good for you," was the general response.

After school we all went down to the café. It was Jaimini's turn to work so the rest of us went in through the main café entrance. The very first person I saw was the little French girl, Marine. Today she was sitting with a woman I didn't know, another little girl and a little boy. Putting two and two together I figured that this was another mother "doing her bit", trying to get Marine to unwind a bit and communicate.

There was a huge chocolate ice-cream sitting on the table in front of her, which looked as though it hadn't been touched. The other two children had empty ice-cream glasses, those tall thin ones, which showed they must have eaten their way through quite a lot, but despite that they were both eyeing up Marine's ice-cream. None of the three children was talking, but the mother was leaning back in her chair, chatting to someone she obviously knew at the table behind her.

As we all sat down at our table on the other side of the café, I heard the mother say in a loud clear voice that people often use when speaking to foreigners, "Ice-cream, Marine? Yum yum!" Then she made smacking lips noises. Marine looked at her as though she was demented, then looked down into her lap. Immediately the other two children started an argument about who should get to eat Marine's ice-cream. The mother spooned it equally into their two glasses, then tried again with Marine.

"Would you like something different?"

I suddenly realized I'd been staring at this little scene for rather a long time because Leah was tapping my leg. "What's so interesting, Andy?" she asked me. The others leaned forward to hear about it too, so I told them briefly about Fen's mum the day before.

"Oh yeah, she was telling Dad about a little French girl," Fen said. "She doesn't look seven, does she?" Tash and Luce turned round to see what they thought, and that's when Marine's eyes met mine.

"*Salut*," I called with a little wave. Her hand rose slowly and she returned my wave, just as she had done the previous day, but there was no smile to go with it.

26

"Andy's got that look on her face," Fen said.

"What look?" I asked.

"The look that says I'm going to crack that problem," Luce informed me. I must have been wearing a puzzled expression.

"You've made a decision to get that little girl to talk, haven't you?" Leah asked me.

I had to smile. They'd got it in one. "I'll go over and chat for a while," I said. "If I do that every time I see her I'm sure to get through to her in the end, aren't I?"

So over I went to introduce myself to the lady. Her name was Mrs Kelly and she seemed pleased and relieved to see me. Marine didn't react at all.

"I'm about at my wits' end," Mrs Kelly told me in a loud whisper. "The child seemed to want to come here, because I made various suggestions about what the children could do – play in the park, have a picnic, play in the garden – and she didn't react to any of them. I wasn't sure if she'd understood a single word I'd said… 'Or we could go and have an ice-cream in the café', I finished off, and she looked up at me and gave the faintest of nods. Yet now we're here she hasn't even touched her ice-cream."

"*Tu n'aimes pas la glace, Marine, ou tu n'as pas faim?*" I asked her, trying to find out whether she simply wasn't hungry.

No answer. No reaction.

27

"She don't understand 'cos she's foreign," the boy informed me.

"She's half French and half English," I explained to the boy, then I turned back to Marine. "*Demande à maman de t'accompagner ici demain. Je voudrais bien la rencontrer.*"

Still no answer, but her eyes looked thoughtful. I'd suggested to her that she ask her mother to bring her to the café the following day. I explained this to Mrs Kelly, then went back to my table. I could see our drinks had arrived.

"*A demain*," (see you tomorrow) I said to Marine.

No reply.

"You've got your work cut out there," Fen commented drily as I sat down. I was about to reply when Jaimini appeared, looking anxious. I sensed that her anxiety would in some way be connected with me.

"Andy, I'm sorry, but we've had a phone call from your mum. Your dad's here."

"Here! Where?" I asked, frantically craning my neck round.

"No, not exactly here. At your house," Jaimini explained.

"But why?" I wanted to know.

Jaimini gave me a sort of apologetic shrug for an answer. A wave of despondency swept over our little group. Personally I felt quite worried. Dad wasn't expected home yet for quite a few days and he hardly ever surprised us like this. I presumed Mum must have told him I was making a fuss about staying with Grandma Sorrell, and Dad was coming home to deal with me personally.

"Your mum wants you back home," Jaimini said, but I was already standing up.

"Don't let him get you down," Luce said bracingly. "Just tell him firmly that Leah's mum has invited you to stay at her place."

"Yes, and make sure he realizes that that would be much less disruptive all round and Grandma Sorrell wouldn't have the worry of waiting for you to come home every day," Tash added logically.

"I'll get Mum to phone your mum, shall I?" Leah suggested.

"Good idea," Fen said. "The sooner the better."

"Won't that make him cross because you've deliberately tried to alter his arrangements?" Jaimini asked, understanding better than any of them the difficulties involved with having a father like mine.

"Jaimini's right. I won't say anything," I muttered thoughtfully, "but get your mum to phone as soon as possible, Leah."

"OK. I'm on my way," Leah said, plonking the money for her Coke on the table and rushing out of the café before me. I started fumbling in my pocket but Fen said she'd pay for me.

"I'll pay you back tomorrow," was my parting shot. I was about to go out of the door when something stopped me. I had completely forgotten about Marine. I turned round and sure enough her big eyes had followed me to the door. Her hand was waving. Her face wore that "nearly" smile.

"*Salut*, Marine," I called with a grin, then I was gone, feeling a tiny streak of optimism lifting my downcast feelings, because she had been first to wave.

I ran all the way home and got a new attack of nerves at the sight of Dad's car in the drive. It made me cross that such a stupid little thing could have that effect on me. "Right Andy, snap out of it," I told myself firmly. "You're going to go in there and tell him calmly but firmly that staying with Grandma Sorrell would be fraught with problems."

With this resolution in mind I went in the house. I could hear Sebastien's voice in the kitchen, so that's where I went first. Mum and Dad were sitting at the table. Sebastien was walking round the table holding on to chairs. Dad stood up and I went over to him. He kissed me on both cheeks which is what he always does when he's just come back from work in France.

Sebastien spotted me and said, "Ada ada ada ada adee!" as his little knees bent then snapped tight over and over again. For some reason or other he was very pleased to see me, and this was the first time he'd ever said anything resembling my name. I scooped him up and gave him kisses but he pulled away and wanted to get down immediately. Typical! Just when I needed a big cuddle Sebastien wasn't interested. Of course, the moment he was back down on the floor his arms went out to me as if to say, "Pick me up, I really mean it this time."

I was secretly rather pleased to have this diversion. "One more chance, buddy," I said jokingly as I picked him up. This time he nestled into me so I sat down at the table with him. He squirmed round to try to get his bottle which was near me. I held the bottle and watched him as he sucked greedily. Good. This way I didn't have to look at Dad.

"You're spending a lot of time at that café these days." Dad launched in with the very line of attack I wanted to leave till last.

"Everybody goes there, Dad. We don't stay long…"

"It can't be doing your school work any favours."

"My homework is always done and it's always handed in on time," I replied as calmly as I could. I still didn't look at him.

"Your mother tells me you are averse to staying with Grandma Sorrell while we are … away."

"I can't see it being very practical," I answered, making myself look at him for the first time.

"Sometimes we have to sacrifice a bit of practicality for other things."

"Such as what?" I quickly countered.

"Such as our peace of mind," he answered, raising his eyebrows and lowering his head slightly as if to say, "You hadn't thought of that, had you?"

"Why wouldn't you have peace of mind if I stayed with Pat?"

The moment the words were out I could have bitten my tongue. Stupid girl, Andy, I thought. You're not supposed to mention Leah's invitation yet. It was at that precise moment that the phone rang. Mum got up to answer it.

"You have somewhere else in mind to stay?" Dad asked me. His expression really got to me. It was as though he was mocking me, giving me a chance to put my case over in the full knowledge that he would win the argument because he always did.

"'Allo," said Mum. "Oh 'allo Pat." There was a long pause then, while Dad and I both watched the frown on Mum's face deepening. Come on Pat, I thought, make a really good case. Pat, as you will have gathered, is Leah's mum. She's very down to earth and ordinary. I prayed that she was saying all the right things. The trouble was, of course, that Mum would ask Dad's opinion because she rarely made decisions like that on her own.

"That's very kind of you indeed," Mum was saying, "but we have already made arrangements for Agnès to go to her grandmuzzer." There was another pause while Mum frowned again, then she said, "Yes … yes … OK. I weel talk to my husband and see what he says. We don't want to offend Agnès' grandmuzzer…" There was another pause, then Mum said, "Yes, of course. I will phone you back if we change our minds, but thank you very much indeed for such a kind offer … goodbye now."

Mum turned to Dad. "Leah's muzzer has offered to have Agnès, *cheri*."

I could tell Mum wouldn't mind if I stayed there. The problem would be persuading Dad. "Oh, that would be great, Mum," I said enthusiastically. "And you'd know I was safely at home at Leah's after school each day because she has so much practice to do."

Mum said, "Yes," in a rather vague way which simply meant, "Ask your father."

"And was Leah practising after school today?" Dad asked me. I considered lying, but knowing him he'd probably find out. My tiny hesitation

33

gave him his answer. I must have looked a bit embarrassed because again he gave me that raised eyebrows look.

"I'm sorry, Agnès," he said, going for the kill, "but the arrangements have been made. Your mother and I can keep in constant touch with Grandma Sorrell and we'll both feel much happier knowing you are not gallivanting about all over the place. You'll just have to forget the café for a while. I'm still not entirely happy about you working there anyway. You never know what kind of people may come into a place like that…"

"But Dad," I interrupted, raising my voice in exasperation and hopelessness, "I don't get it. How come I'm allowed to work there all the time you're away, and now, just because Mum's away too, I'm suddenly not allowed any more…"

"For that very reason. Because your mother will be away too. While one parent is overseeing your actions there is no problem, but Grandma Sorrell, while prepared to look after you, is not prepared to have the further responsibility and worry of never knowing what time you're going to be home."

"But I could phone her."

"I have said no, Agnès."

He stood up abruptly and glared at me. I wanted to kick him hard, for being so strict, then shake Mum hard for being so weak and not sticking up for me. Dad strode out of the room and Mum gave me one of her semi-apologetic looks, the sort that meant, *I'm sorry for you Andy, I almost agree with you, but actually when the chips are down, I must agree with your father.*

"You'd better get packed, *bibiche*. I'll help you," she said softly.

"Packed! Now? Why?"

"We leave tomorrow."

She put her arm round me and it was a good job she did because I nearly fell over with shock at this latest revelation.

"I didn't realize you were going so soon," I said.

Her arm tightened round my shoulder and she drew me to her. I could tell she felt really sorry for me.

"I weesh I deedn't have to go Agnès, but…"

"Well, don't go then, Mum," I said with one last desperate plea. "If you don't really want to go, you don't have to, you know." It was like our roles were being reversed for a moment.

"It's not so easy as that," she answered with a sigh. "I *do* have to go." She suddenly turned brisk and positive. "Come on, let's get packing. The sooner we go, the sooner we come back."

There was no more point in protesting. I'd said all I could. I just had to accept the situation for the moment. I didn't want to create trouble between Mum and Dad. I've been in these no-win situations before and the only way to deal with them is to make the very best you can of them and just hope the time will go quickly.

"Can I have a telephone number where I can contact you, Mum?" I asked her in the middle of the packing. Again I noticed her eyes doing that fluttering thing.

"We'll be travelling around quite a bit at first … but as soon as we can we'll give you a number. Until then, we'll phone you."

Something funny was going on and I was determined to find out what. I was also getting ideas flashing through my mind about how to go to the café without Grandma Sorrell being any wiser. I tried to shake these thoughts away before they were able to take root in my brain, and start growing into full-scale plans. Because once I get an idea that only needs courage to carry out, I have to do it. Something makes me. That's how I got my name – the daring one.

The next day at morning break we were all down at the bottom of the netball courts again. There had been a lot of wide-eyed, indignant, open-mouthed looks as I told them about last night's conversation. "Thank your mum for trying," I said to Leah. "If only I'd had a bit more warning we could have made a better case out of it, but it was a non-starter from the word go, because Dad never goes back on his arrangements."

"So today you've got to go on the bus to Grandma Sorrell's?" asked Fen.

I nodded miserably.

"And tomorrow and the next day?" Luce put in to really cheer me up. Jaimini gave her friend a nudge with her elbow but Luce was not to be stopped. "And what about the weekend? Surely you're not going to be cloistered up all weekend as well?"

"I'm going to Grandma Sorrell's on the bus today, because it's the first day," I told them. "But tomorrow, I don't know. Tomorrow I'll think again."

My eyes must have been glinting or something.

"She's got that look on her face," Fen said. "Go for it, Andy! Break out!" The others all nodded with wicked smiles. "Yeah, break out!" they agreed.

"Do you want one of us to come back with you on the bus today?" Tash asked kindly.

"No, don't worry, I'll be OK."

The bus to Grandma Sorrell's house was maroon and brown. There were quite a lot of kids from our school on it, including some year-ten boys who were sitting at the back and making loud stupid jokes, about the year sevens mainly. The year sevens sat at the front and just ignored the remarks. They were obviously used to it. But there was one girl who was sitting on her own and looked very uncomfortable.

Really, as a year eight I should have tried to get a seat a bit further back, but there were only three other year eights on the bus and they were all boys. So I had the choice between sitting next to a boy, which would really stir up the year-ten comments, or sitting next to the worried looking year-seven girl. There were some seats just in front of the year tens at the back, but I decided against that as it was my first day.

"We don't have primary school kids on this bus," called out one of the boys from the back.

"You'd better get off then," I retorted, standing up to face him for a moment. As I spoke I was aware of the girl beside me tensing up as though I was about to be shot or something for speaking like that. Either she's very unsure of herself or these boys are really horrible, I thought to myself. Loads of laughing and shrieking followed which wasn't aimed at anyone in particular so I turned to the girl next to me.

"I'm Andy," I said.

"I'm Mandy," she answered, and we both smiled because our names were so similar.

"What's your real name?" she wanted to know.

"Agnès. It's French, you see," I explained.

"Oh… Are you always going to come on this bus?"

"For a while, most days, yeah."

"Oh, good."

We chatted away about school and teachers and horrible year-ten boys, and I explained about my grandmother and my parents being away.

"We'll be getting off at the same stop," Mandy said, her eyes lighting up. "It'll be absolutely brilliant to have someone to stand with at the bus stop. I can't tell you how awful it is with those boys around."

She seemed so grateful that I was there that I felt sure she must have been exaggerating, but a moment later I was proved wrong.

Chapter 3

As if on cue, one of the boys suddenly started to sing to the tune of Baa Baa Black Sheep:

"Mouldy Mandy, what a stupid twit, not a girl but just an 'it'." At this point all the boys joined in: "Mouldy Mandy's plastic mum, plastic boobs and plastic bum, mouldy Mandy, what a stupid twit, not a girl but just an 'it'."

I felt my blood boiling as I saw tears pricking at the corners of Mandy's eyes.

"Have they only just made that up?" I asked her quickly.

She shook her head and one of the tears fell out. "When you see Mum you'll see why they sing it, but she's never had any plastic surgery, never once. She just happens to be really nice-looking. I wish she wasn't, I really do." Poor Mandy had about broken down into tears. I got up quickly and walked down to the driver at the front.

"Did you hear that?" I asked him.

"What's that, love?"

"That song that those boys just sung."

The driver was obviously used to the boys, and either past caring or too lazy to make much effort.

"That's enough of that you lot," he bellowed out, but it didn't have any effect on the boys. I sat down again, knowing immediately that I'd made matters worse, because drivers aren't like teachers and it's not really their responsibility to tell kids off.

"You get good, jokey bus drivers, and quiet ones," Mandy explained, "but not many of them do any good against all those boys."

"Diddums told de man about de boys, did she. Ah, poor little diddums!" came a nasty voice from the back.

"How pathetic," someone else sneered.

"What's 'er name anyway?" asked someone else.

"She's got some weird name," replied another voice.

"My name's Andy," I called out. I was about to add that I didn't put up with low-life like them, but the moment I'd said my name they all broke into chants of "Andy Pandy's coming to play", which quickly got changed to "Andy and Mandy are coming to play…"

"Just ignore them," one of the sensible year-

41

nine girls advised me. I glanced around. The rest of the bus was certainly ignoring them. I couldn't decide whether or not this was through boredom at hearing the same loud, aggressive voices mouthing off every day, or whether the rest of the kids had got wise and decided it was safer not to meddle, not even to react.

Mandy and I got off at our stop. Personally, I practically fell off, because one of the year-ten boys who was also getting off knocked so hard into me. The boys – there were three of them getting off at the same stop – disappeared immediately, which just left four people at the bus stop: me, Mandy, Grandma Sorrell and Mandy's mum.

I knew I should have been greeting Grandma Sorrell and receiving one of her dry-lipped kisses, but all I could do was stare at Mandy's mum. Her hair was shiny, thick and blonde, tumbling on to her golden brown shoulders. It was quite a hot day and she was wearing a tight T-shirt and an even tighter short skirt. She looked like something out of Baywatch.

Realizing suddenly that I was staring, I gave her a quick "hello", and then with a quick "bye" and "see you tomorrow" to Mandy, I turned to Grandma Sorrell. It was several weeks since I'd seen her, but we didn't hug each other because we never did. It wasn't her style. She probably didn't know how to hug!

"Small as ever I see," she commented, leaning forwards about two centimetres, which I think was my cue to kiss her papery cheek. I dutifully did this, then asked in polite tones how she was.

"None the better for standing here for ten minutes," she replied, turning to walk back home. I meekly followed, feeling a huge cloud of depression hanging over me.

"Homework?" was her next charming conversation piece.

"I did my maths at dinnertime so I've only got science," I replied as politely as I could.

"Only two subjects?" she snapped, turning her head, as if by looking at me she could check whether I was telling the truth.

"It's always two or three," I explained wearily. We were walking so slowly. I could hardly bear it.

"Do you mind if I run on ahead?" I asked her impulsively.

"If it makes you happy," she replied, sounding irritated and surprised at the same time.

I was about to thrust my school bag at her so I could really run, but I decided that that wouldn't go down very well so I ran with the bag banging against my hip at every step.

After a while I passed one of the year-ten boys. The other two must have gone off in different directions or already reached their houses. This boy didn't make any comment at all as I passed him. Huh, not so brave without your mates, I thought. And that made me feel even more depressed. I wished more than anything in the world that I was in the café with *my* friends at that moment, and that Mum and Dad had changed their minds and weren't going away after all.

Grandma Sorrell's big old house stood gauntly behind a high hedge. It was pretty isolated. The neighbouring house was about twenty-five metres away and also hidden behind a hedge. I looked in to the drive as I ran past it, though, and a plump, smiley woman in her fifties I guess, called out "Someone's in a hurry." I smiled at her as she snipped some dead heads off her flowers.

At Grandma Sorrell's house I walked up to the front door and sat on the doorstep staring at the garden. Even the flowers looked as though they'd been specially selected for their dullness. They were mauve and white, clumpy and straggly, and where the soil showed it was dry and grey. I heaved a sigh as Grandma Sorrell appeared.

"Don't sit on the step. You'll get piles." I got up obediently and thought, No wonder Dad is as he is, with this tyrannical old bag for a mother. She had her front door key all ready and in she marched. "What's the name of your neighbour?" I asked conversationally.

"Mrs Hatch, and she's a busybody."

So that was the end of that conversation. Instead of talking I started staring round me at the big, rich, old-ladyish house. It was ages since I'd been there because we didn't see Grandma Sorrell all that often, and when we did see her it was generally at our house. First we came to the hall where I dropped my bag out of force of habit on to the bare polished floorboards.

"Not there!" she snapped. "Follow me."

We went up the very wide staircase which was carpeted in dark red and had brass stair rods. Even with the carpet there was still some dark wooden stair showing at each end of every step. The house got darker the higher we went. I bet I'm going to just love my bedroom, I thought. I'd been upstairs in this house when Grandpa had been alive, but not very often because I used to find it quite dark and scary when I was younger.

The landing had two dull, dark bookcases in it. The title *Bleak House* leapt out at me, a book by Charles Dickens. How appropriate, I thought.

"I expect you to make your bed and keep your room tidy," Grandma Sorrell said, thrusting open the door at the end. There were two doors on the right of the landing and three on the left. All five doors were dark and closed.

Surprisingly, my room wasn't bad. The window looked out on the garden at the back which was big and had a stone wall all along one side. There were some huge dark trees at the end of it, but they were too far from my window to darken my room. The bed, which was a double one, was very high and bumpy-looking, with a dark blue, heavily embroidered cover over it. I was dying for Grandma Sorrell to go so I could look and see what lay underneath this cover. Nothing would have surprised me – a sack of potatoes, writhing snakes, a couple of corpses – nothing.

She was standing there as though waiting for a tip or something. I looked at her. "The basin is there," she finally said, pointing to the white old-fashioned basin with its small square mirror, in the corner of the room. "...but the toilet –" she turned from the room so I followed – "is here."

It was the third door on the left which she thrust open. This was a very narrow room, like a little corridor with a white loo and a dark brown cover. The cistern, high above it, was also dark brown. Apart from that there was just a tiny washbasin in this room, as well as a little towel rail, a waste-paper bin and something on the wall that I can't call a picture, because it was just lines from the Bible in a frame.

"Thank you," I said not knowing what else to say.

She nodded curtly. "I expect your homework to

be your first task on returning from school. We eat at six as a rule."

Then off she walked, tall and stiff. I went back to my bedroom, shut the door behind me and peeled back the bed cover in one aggressive sweep. I think Grandma Sorrell must have been to evening classes in tight bed-making. I yanked out the sides and flapped them about a bit, then heaved open the curved drawers of the mahogany chest. They were lined with brown paper.

I cautiously opened the wardrobe door to see a few dangling coat hangers and a full-length mirror in the door. My enormous squashy purple bag sat on the floor at the side of the wardrobe. Mum and Dad had delivered it while I was at school. It looked wrong in this room, too bright and modern. I unzipped it just enough to see that Mum had stuck Herman on top of all my clothes. Herman is my Gorilla. He's golden brown with rather matted hair. I picked him up, curled up in the chair and cuddled him.

After about ten seconds I gave myself and Herman a good talking to. "Right," I said, holding him at arm's length and addressing his gooey gorilla eyes. "We're not going to let this house get us down, OK? And neither are we going to let Grandma Sorrell get to us. We're going to make the very best of this situation, escaping at every opportunity, and pleading with Mum on the phone to make Dad change his mind and let me stay at Leah's. Only we won't plead too much because we don't want to worry her. And the very first thing we're going to do, Herman, is this…"

I got out my science exercise book, tore out the middle pages and made a chart of twenty-one days which I put in the bottom drawer of the desk, then I got on with my homework. After five minutes of staring at the science experiment I'd done that day, and trying to write a conclusion, I realized my brain was on other things. Stuffing Herman down my jumper, I tiptoed to the door, opened it, then crept to the top of the stairs and peered down to check that Grandma Sorrell wasn't keeping watch from below. There was no sign of her, not even a sound of her, so goodness knows what she was doing down there.

I tried the first door on the left of the landing but it wouldn't open. I pushed it as hard as I dared but it must have been locked. My heart started beating faster because this seemed very mysterious. The next door opened easily to reveal a bathroom. The bath, basin and toilet were all white, and the carpet, curtains and walls were all different shades of green. This room must have been for Grandma Sorrell's personal use. That's why she had shown me the other loo. Perhaps I wasn't allowed a bath. It didn't bother me. I didn't fancy getting into a bath that her flaky skin had been in. But I did wish she had a shower. I love showers, especially when I've been running.

The room next to mine was also a bedroom which looked like another spare room, but the room next to that, which was opposite Grandma Sorrell's, was also locked. Weird. The sound of footsteps downstairs made me dive back into my own room and plunge back into my science, which I finished in ten minutes.

As I changed and unpacked all my clothes, and put Herman on the bed, I felt more and more gloomy. There was no way I was going to be able to put up with this for three weeks. It felt like being a prisoner, and I was also angry with Mum and Dad for landing me in this situation. I was jealous of Sebastien for being allowed to stay with Mami and Papi. It was obvious why of course, because he didn't go to school and I did. Anyway, Grandma Sorrell could no more have looked after Sebastien than she could have managed to keep a couple of lions.

I marched purposefully downstairs and heard the phone ringing. It was a very loud ring which stopped when I'd reached the hall, so I went towards the sitting room where I knew the phone was kept. As I opened the door Grandma Sorrell said, "Just a minute," rather curtly into the mouthpiece, then looked at me as if to say, "Yes? What do you want in my private apartment?"

"I'm just going out for a walk," I answered her impulsively. She looked a bit taken aback but was probably glad to get rid of me.

"Don't go far and don't forget tea at six."

Off I went. At least I wasn't going to be kept a total prisoner. A surge of optimism hit me as I ran towards the bus stop where there was a telephone. I pressed a twenty-pence piece into the slot and dialled Leah's number. Kim answered but Leah quickly came on the phone.

"Hi, how's it going?" she asked, in such a sympathetic voice I nearly burst into tears.

"It's awful," I told her. "Grandma Sorrell seems more horrible than ever. I've rechristened her house Bleak House. There's absolutely nothing for me to do there. I'll go round the twist if I have to stay much longer."

"Oh Andy, I'm really sorry. You'll just have to tell your mum how awful it is and beg her to let you come and stay with me."

"The trouble is I might not get the chance to talk to her privately with Grandma Sorrell around all the time."

"We'll all get together tomorrow and sort out a plan," Leah said, knowing that that sort of positive talk would cheer me up. "Fen'll think of something. You know what she's like!"

"Yeah, OK. I'd better go now, Leah. See you tomorrow."

"Good luck."

"Thanks. Bye."

So the following morning we were down on the netball courts yet again and I was giving the others the full horror story in graphic detail, including the bus journey with poor Mandy who had suffered more insults on the way to school that morning.

"That's the one and only good thing about all this," I said. "Mandy is so relieved to have someone to stick up for her."

"What was it like when you got back from phoning me?" Leah asked.

"Torture. Grandma Sorrell doesn't approve of too much television so we listened to the radio, then she asked me whether or not I had a good book to read. If I hadn't been so miserable I would have laughed."

"Did your mum ring?" Tash asked.

"No, Grandma Sorrell said she didn't think they'd ring that first evening because they probably wouldn't be there yet. The weird thing is," I went on, "that the old bag doesn't really seem to want me there. I got the definite feeling that she'd let me stay the night at your place Leah, if I handled it properly."

"Yeah?" Leah's eyes lit up. "Why not ask her for tomorrow night, Saturday? Then you could get away for more or less the whole weekend."

"OK, I'll try it."

"I know somebody who's desperate to see you," Fen suddenly said.

I looked at her and instantly knew. "Marine?"

"Yes. It was my turn at the café yesterday and Marine was there with her mum."

"I'd completely forgotten about that," I said, feeling guilty.

"Her mum asked me if Andy was around anywhere. I explained that you were staying at your grandma's for three weeks and possibly wouldn't be able to come to the café. Marine didn't exactly burst into tears but she looked pretty downcast."

"Oh, poor little kid," I said. "I've got to try and see her."

"Tomorrow you'll be at my place, remember. We'll go to the café in the afternoon," Leah said.

"It's Yours Truly holding the fort tomorrow," said Luce, standing up and bowing to left and right.

Jaimini yanked her down and then said sensibly, "The trouble is if Fen's told her you won't be there…"

"It's OK. I can get their number from Rachel's school," Fen replied.

"Why don't you come to the café today, Andy?" Luce asked with a wicked grin.

"It's tempting, but if I turn up late today I

might not get to stay the night with Leah tomorrow."

The others nodded – realizing that I'd made a sensible decision, but what they didn't realize was that part of the reason for my decision was Mandy. I couldn't bear to think of her being alone at the front of that bus with the jeering boys mocking her the whole time.

I didn't concentrate much for the rest of the morning at school because I felt pulled at from all directions. On the one side there was Marine and on the other Mandy. And then there was Grandma Sorrell. Was she pulling? Or was she actually pushing? Something wasn't adding up. Across my mind shot a picture of her covering the mouthpiece when I went into the sitting room and interrupted her phone call. And what about the locked doors and my feeling that she didn't really want me there?

By lunchtime I'd hatched a terrific plan.

"Leah," I said excitedly, "why don't you come and stay with me tonight? I'll phone Grandma Sorrell. I'm sure she can't object to that."

"Yeah, OK. That would be great," Leah answered enthusiastically.

"Lucky thing, you'll get to see Bleak House and Grumpy Snotbag," Luce put in, which made us all laugh.

So Leah phoned her mum right there and then

from school and her mum said that was fine. She even agreed to drop in an overnight bag at the end of school so Leah could come straight on the bus with me.

"Just Grandma Sorrell to phone now," I said, punching in the number. She answered after only one ring.

"Lesley?" she said, sounding surprised. That really threw me, I can tell you. Who on earth was Lesley?

"It's me, Grandma Sorrell. Andy."

"Oh, Agnès … yes?"

"I was wondering if I could have my friend Leah to stay the night tonight. She's really nice and quiet," I added.

"Not tonight, Agnès."

"Oh, *please…*"

"I'm sorry, no. Not tonight." There was something very definite in her voice and I knew there was no point in pursuing it. "Perhaps one day next week," she added after a pause.

"See you later then," I said in a flat voice, and put the phone down.

"I presume she said no," said Leah quietly.

I nodded. "But why do you think she said 'Not tonight' in such a decisive manner as if she wouldn't really mind any other night?"

"Maybe she's got something planned for just the two of you," Tash said fancifully.

"Yeah, perhaps she's going to order two big pizzas and hire a good video," Jaimini went on cheerfully.

"And maybe the English Channel will freeze over at the same time," I said sarcastically.

"I think you ought to go ahead anyway," commented Luce casually as she examined the ends of Jaimini's hair, which she was always doing.

"Go ahead with what?" Fen asked.

"Have Leah to stay."

There was a brief silence while we examined this possibility from every angle, then Tash spoke, wide-eyed, "What? Smuggle her in?"

"Yeah, why not?" Luce answered. After another short silence it was me who spoke because the usual thing had happened. Luce's idea had taken root in my mind, and once that happens there's no turning back.

"Go on, Leah, it would be so exciting. Let's try it!"

Leah was looking very worried and no wonder. She was the biggest worrier of us all and here I was expecting her to go along with this really daring idea.

"What if she discovered I was there? She'd probably kill me or something."

"She won't discover you, honestly. It'll be brilliant ... *pleeeeease*," I pleaded. "It'll be so mega creeping round spying on her, and you don't want me to suffer another boring evening, do you?"

"That's emotional blackmail," Leah answered, but she was smiling and I knew she was cracking. "All right," she finally said.

"Yessss!" I said, punching the air, while all the others jumped up and down like a bunch of little kids.

"I don't know what we're excited about," said Tash, calming down first. "Anyone would think we're *all* going to be smuggled in."

"Yes, why don't we?" Luce began, eyes shining.

"Absolutely not." Jaimini squashed Luce before she could get any further along those ridiculous lines.

"What about food?" Leah asked practically.

"I'll smuggle food up to you from the pantry. We'll have a midnight feast."

We carried on talking excitedly until the end of lunch break, then all through the afternoon my mind kept coming back to what lay in store – exciting but a bit scary – my favourite kind of adventure!

Chapter 4

After school, Leah's mum delivered the overnight bag as promised, and off we went to get the bus. Tash was working at the café, but the others all came to see us off at the bus stop. The year-ten boys were already at the back of the bus. They were about to start making pathetic comments about Andy and Mandy when they saw me get on with Leah. This had the instant effect of making them lost for words because all boys think Leah is a wow.

We sat down next to Mandy, squashing three on a seat, and immediately told her what we were up to. Her eyes danced excitedly with that look that appears in anyone's eyes who's listening to a wicked plan and knowing that they're not going to be involved themselves, so there's nothing to fear.

"Brought a little friend, have we?" one of the

boys from the back called down the bus in a deliberately babyish voice. They'd obviously recovered from the initial shock of seeing Leah.

"I don't know. Have you?" I retorted, standing up and turning round because he didn't scare me one iota.

Mandy immediately pulled me back down and hissed, "Don't answer back, Andy, he'll go mad." Before I had been hauled back into my seat, I caught the anxious looks on the faces of the year-nine and ten girls, and one of the year-tens even gave me the tiniest shake of her head as if to say, "I shouldn't if I were you."

"Even the year-ten girls are scared of those boys," Mandy said, telling me what I'd just sussed. "And there's a reason too." Leah and I leaned towards Mandy to hear what was coming next. "People say that his dad's violent and that Darren's inherited it," she confided in a whisper.

"Well, he doesn't scare me," I replied, because he didn't. There'd been a boy called Gary Barker at our school who'd been the ring leader of that lot, but he'd been expelled eventually, and the new ring leader was the boy who had just spoken to me. His name was Darren Kirk and he was tall, quite dark, rather hunched – or maybe that was just the way he was always sitting – and he wore a very hard expression on his face the whole time.

"Omigod! He's coming down here," Mandy

said, clutching my arm, which was ridiculous because she was much bigger than me.

"Oh, Andy," Leah whispered, sounding terrified.

I looked up to see Darren Kirk towering over me menacingly. I don't know why he didn't scare me but he didn't. Maybe it was living with my dad for thirteen years, because as far as I was concerned there was much more behind my dad's scariness.

"Did you say something, kid?" he asked in a slow threatening voice.

"Yes, I did. I answered you back, Darren." I replied coolly while the rest of the bus listened in open-mouthed silence. "I know you're not used to people answering you back, but it's really a perfectly natural thing. People do it hundreds of times a day," I went on sarcastically. I must admit my heart was beating rather faster by then because I seemed to have gained the attention of the whole bus for some reason. I could practically feel Mandy and Leah flinching like little toddlers do when they know they've been naughty and their mum's about to give them a smack.

Darren was just staring at me, obviously weighing up what to do or say, when something very unusual happened. The driver stopped the bus and stood up. It was a different driver from yesterday. This was a woman – MRS PAYNE, her badge said. She was about forty-five, quite stern-looking, fairly large and she wore glasses with purple frames.

"Get back to your place," she said, in an icy-cold voice, pointing to the back of the bus while boring a hole in Darren's face with the intensity of her look.

"She started it," he began almost whining.

"No she didn't, you big bully. You started it. Get back to your place. Now! Go!"

Darren had no choice. He ambled off, mumbling under his breath as though that might save him a bit of cool, but it didn't because most of the girls on the bus giggled openly as he went past them. The driver returned to her seat, face still looking like thunder.

"Brilliant," Mandy told me with feeling.

Leah just let out her breath in a long sigh of relief, and said, "I'm not sure I'm looking forward to tonight with you around, Andy," which made us all laugh.

The rest of the bus journey was uneventful. The boys at the back made sure they laughed loudly a lot, as if to show that Darren's telling-off hadn't had any effect on them really. The only other nasty thing happened as we were getting off at our stop. Darren got himself right next to me, and without appearing to move his lips at all, said, "You just wait till Monday. You won't have

Mrs Hitler to protect you then, you know."

A small tremor of fear passed through me, but I quickly decided to cross that bridge when I came to it. Before that, I'd got a whole weekend with, hopefully, quite a bit of freedom.

"Where is she?" Leah asked as she looked all round for Grandma Sorrell. Mandy's mum gave us a friendly wave, and we said "Bye" to her and to Mandy. "See you Monday," I called as they went off together.

"Her mum's really attractive," Leah breathed, staring after the two of them.

The boys had sidled away quickly again, so Leah and I were left alone, which was slightly confusing because we'd planned to say goodbye to each other, and then for Leah to walk several paces behind all the way to Bleak House, then wait outside, hidden by the hedge, until I came out to get her and smuggle her in as soon as the coast was clear.

As there was no sign of Grandma Sorrell we decided to walk together, and then, if she appeared, we'd make a big thing of saying "Bye" to each other, and Leah would hang back and catch up later. As it happened we got all the way to Bleak House and still there was no sign of her.

"Stay here, I'll come out for you as soon as possible," I whispered. She nodded, big-eyed. I decided to try the back door. It was open so I went in quickly. I could have called out but I decided it would be more interesting to creep silently. When I had reached the end of the back lobby, as Grandma Sorrell called the little corridor at the back, I heard her voice.

It didn't take a moment for me to realize she was on the phone, though I couldn't work out what she was saying. Hoping it wouldn't creak or anything, I gently turned the knob of the door through to the front hall. It opened smoothly so I tiptoed towards the sitting room. I began to distinguish the odd word that she was saying like "matters" and "granddaughter" which set my imagination working, of course.

Thinking that this would be a good time to smuggle Leah in, I nipped back out the way I'd come in, not bothering to shut the middle door. Leah moved more noisily than I did and kept on having to smother nervous giggles. I went on ahead of her to check that Grandma Sorrell was still on the phone, then led the way up the stair-case and into my room, where we both collapsed in a fit of laughter.

A moment later we were jolted into silence by the sound of the dreaded voice approaching, "Agnès?" We froze.

"Quick, it's her! Get in the wardrobe," I whispered urgently.

Leah got in amongst my clothes and crouched

down. I shut the door, then saw her bag sitting in the middle of the floor, tried to stuff it under the bed, but it wouldn't go, so left it tucked in at the side of the bed hidden from the door, and chucked my dressing gown on top of it, then opened the door and walked across the landing.

"Hello, Grandma Sorrell," I called brightly as she mounted the last two stairs. She was peering at me as though she knew something was going on, but couldn't quite work out what, and thought the answer might be written on my face. "Just putting my school bag away," I said casually. "I didn't want to disturb you because I knew you were on the phone," I added.

"Wretched thing rang as I was on the point of leaving for the bus stop."

"You don't have to meet me at the bus stop, Grandma Sorrell. I can easily walk home by myself."

She did a sort of soft grunt which could have been interpreted as a yes or a no, then asked if I had homework.

"Yes, but I've got the whole weekend to do it in."

"As long as you're staying in this house, I want homework out of the way immediately. Your father always used to do his homework the moment he got home, you know."

"Then what did he do afterwards?" I asked,

which threw her slightly.

"O-oh, he read a book, or played with a football in the garden…"

"Didn't he have any friends?" I asked, pressing her to try and reveal that Dad must have had at least a bit of pleasure in his dull-sounding child-hood at Bleak House.

"There was a young lad who lived a few minutes away from here who he used to see some-times." I waited but she'd obviously come to the end of Dad's childhood memories because she suddenly said, "We'll eat at five-thirty today. I'll let you get on with your homework now."

We parted ways but I waited for a good thirty seconds before letting Leah out of the wardrobe. She practically fell out, gasping for air and saying, "It is absolutely unbearable in there, Andy. I hope I don't have to spend too much time cramped up in the dark tonight."

At twenty past five I left Leah sitting on the floor on the side of the bed that was hidden from the door, and went downstairs to the kitchen.

"Do you mind if I eat in my room so I can carry on with my homework, Grandma Sorrell? It's a history project and I'm really absorbed in it."

"There are sandwiches, shortcake and an apple," she answered. I noticed she couldn't quite manage to give me praise for my keenness to work hard. I put everything on the tray along with the bottle of lemonade that was out on the side, and the glass. "Just take a tumbler full," she ordered.

"I'm really thirsty, you see, *and* really hungry too," I explained with an apologetic look.

"Well, there are a couple of cold sausages in the fridge if you want them, but I really don't know where you put it all."

Grandma Sorrell was definitely more cheerful this evening, despite her reluctance to show it.

Leah's eyes lit up when she saw that there was plenty for both of us to eat and drink. We also had two bars of chocolate that we'd bought at the school shop at break that day, so we weren't going to starve.

"Do you think she can hear us up here?" Leah asked anxiously.

"No, I'm sure she can't. Anyway, she's got the radio on. Perhaps she'll burst into song in a minute." We were on the point of spluttering on our cheese sandwiches at the thought of this, when to our horror there came a knock at the door.

There was no time for wardrobe manoeuvres so Leah flattened herself on the floor, hidden behind the bed, and I raced to the door, heart pounding.

"I have to go out for a short time," Grandma Sorrell said, peering over my head into the room.

"All right," I said, feeling a mixture of delight at her words, and dreadful nervousness that she might be able to see Leah's foot or something.

"I thought I heard talking," she said sus-piciously. I put on a show of acting embarrassed and said, "Yes, I sometimes say things out loud to see what they sound like before I write them down, you see."

She nodded as though satisfied with this answer.

"When you've finished your project you can watch some television if you want."

"Oh, thanks," I said, but left it at that because I didn't want to say anything that might extend the conversation.

Leah was rather prone to nervous giggles, and if she let one out now it would be curtains for me.

"Goodbye then," murmured Grandma Sorrell rather awkwardly as she turned to go.

It was very tempting to break out in war whoops of delight but we had to contain our joy until she was well and truly out of the house. We listened intently for every sound and eventually heard the front door clicking shut, at which point we crept halfway downstairs and watched through the frosty glass of the stairs window as she climbed stiffly into her small clean car, and drove off.

The sight of the old-fashioned person driving so slowly and jerkily away, and giving us a bit of freedom, prompted a massive outburst of crazy singing and dancing from us. Leah's got a beautiful voice and she sang loads of different pop songs really loudly, while I danced around all over the house, leaping over the sofa and on to the table, and occasionally joined in the singing. We carried on like this until we were shocked into frozen statues by the phone ringing.

"Leave it," Leah promptly advised.

"What if it's Mum?"

"Answer it," Leah said, quickly changing her mind, so I did.

"Hello?" I said, praying for it to be Mum. There was a pause, then the phone at the other end was put down.

"Perhaps it *was* your mum but she couldn't hear you. You often get problems phoning from abroad. Let's see if it rings again." So we waited, staring at it, willing it to ring again, but it never did.

We watched a bit of television, then Leah suggested we phone Tash to see if anything interesting had been going on in the café in our absence. It was Tash's little sister Peta who answered. Peta is only just three and really entertaining, though sometimes quite difficult to get off the phone.

"Hello, vis is Peta Donson speaking. Who is vat speaking?"

"Hi, Peta, it's me – Andy."

"Hello, Andy. Do you want Tash?"

"Yes please, Peta. Could you go and get her?"

This was very successful so far. Perhaps Peta had finally cracked her telephone technique. "She's in ve baaf."

"Oh, could you…" I was about to ask her to get Tash to phone me back but there was a strong risk that the message might not get through. "I'll phone back soon. Has she only just got in or has she been there for quite a while?"

"She's only just got out."

"She's got out!"

At this point I heard her whisper to someone, "It's Andy Pandy." Then I heard Tash's impatient tones. "Well, give me the phone. Let me talk to her." But it wasn't that easy with Peta.

"No," she said, "she's going to phone you back soon."

"Has she gone then?" Tash asked Peta.

"No, not yet," Peta informed her.

At that point Tash must have grabbed the phone from her little sister.

"Andy?" she said.

"Hi," I laughed.

"Sorry about that. How's it going? Did you manage to get Leah in?"

So Leah and I handed the phone to each other, taking it in turns to tell Tash what had happened on the bus and since we'd been at Bleak House. Tash listened with gasps at first and then giggles.

After that I asked her if anything interesting had happened at the café.

"No, not really. Well, only this woman who kept staring at me."

"What was she like?"

"Um, quite ordinary-looking, about fifty-five I guess. Permed hair – a bit blue."

"What about Marine? Was she there?"

"No, 'fraid not. Maybe she'll be there tomorrow. You *are* coming tomorrow, Andy? Have you asked if you can stay with Leah yet?"

"Not yet. I'm waiting till Leah's gone back, otherwise her mum will think it's a bit strange."

We chatted a bit more, then we rang off.

"Did Grandma Sorrell say how long she was going to be?" Leah asked.

"No, and I was so keen to get rid of her I forgot to ask."

We decided to risk watching television with the volume turned down a bit and our ears on stalks for the sound of the front door. We'd already planned what to do when we heard the door go. We would switch off the television and go into the garden through the patio doors which we'd left a teeny bit ajar. Leah would hide behind the rhododendrons and I would pretend to be admiring some other shrubs; then I'd smuggle Leah back in again when the coast was clear. This was the only thing we could do. There wouldn't be time to get upstairs without being caught.

Once our plan was in place we explored the whole house together, finding nothing more interesting than I'd found the previous day. The same two doors on the landing were still locked. We let our imaginations run wild guessing what was behind them, then went downstairs and settled in, ready to watch low-sound telly.

It was well over an hour later when we heard the sound of Grandma Sorrell's key turning in the lock. As fast as we could, and without a sound, we switched off the television and slipped out into the garden where Leah crouched down behind the rhododendron bush. I started strolling around feeling a bit stupid, then, deciding that Grandma Sorrell would find my behaviour pretty suspect, I began turning cartwheels.

"Oh, there you are." She had come out through the patio doors but stopped only just outside. "Have there been any phone calls?"

"Only one, but it must have been a wrong number," I replied cheerfully.

"I hope your homework is all finished?"

"Oh, yes," I assured her.

"Good, I'll have a look at that later." My face drained. "Right, well there's just time for a few games of cards, or maybe you prefer draughts, before you go to bed."

"Bed! But it's only twenty past eight." The moment I said it, I regretted it. After all, the bedroom was exactly where I wanted to be, as Leah and I couldn't go anywhere else in the house.

"By the time we've played some cards it'll be a quarter to nine which isn't unreasonable for a girl of your age."

Cards? How boring. I thought it wiser not to say I wanted to go to bed after all, because she might suspect something. The only other thing I could plead was homework, and that would remind her of my history project which I was praying she'd forget. All the same I did keep getting the feeling that she wanted me out of the way. I'd planned not to ask about staying at Leah's until tomorrow, but on reflection now was definitely a good time to mention it.

"Grandma Sorrell, I was wondering if I could stay at my friend's house tomorrow night?"

I heard a sharp intake of breath from the rhododendron bush.

"Certainly not!" said Grandma Sorrell firmly. But then it was almost as if she regretted answering so hastily, because a thoughtful, hesitant look came over her face. I knew I was right. She wanted to get rid of me. "Which friend? I'll need to speak to her mother, you know," she added, trying for a strict tone.

Again I was aware that there was more to Grandma Sorrell than met the eye. But at that time I couldn't work her out at all. On the one hand she was totally over the top with her old-fashioned principles and her ridiculously strict way of carrying on. But on the other there were chinks in her armour. Mum had once told me that when Grandpa died Grandma Sorrell's heart was broken for weeks and weeks. Then almost overnight there was a huge change in her. Gone was the sad, lonely old lady, and in her place was this formidable hard person.

"She's built a barrier between herself and the rest of the world," Mum had tried to explain to me. "It's the only way she can cope with being on her own now Grandpa's died." Like mother, like son, I thought. Grandma Sorrell and Dad certainly had a lot in common.

"My friend's called Leah Bryan." I answered her question. "But there's no point in phoning this evening," I quickly added, "because the whole family has gone out to the cinema. They won't be back till late."

"In you come then. I want to shut this patio door. It's getting rather chilly."

I did another quick cartwheel by which time she'd turned round so I was able to mouth to Leah, "Back as soon as poss." Leah nodded and looked slightly alarmed, and no wonder. She might be left out there for quite a while.

Changing my mind suddenly about our plan, and seeing that Grandma Sorrell was safely out of earshot, I hissed at Leah, "I'll leave the back door open. Let yourself in in five minutes. I'll make sure the coast is clear."

I followed Grandma Sorrell into the house and shut the patio doors behind me. She was bending down to look into a corner cupboard. "Well what is it to be? Cards or draughts?"

"Cards," I answered, not really caring. "I'll just get my drink."

I slipped away and opened the back door just a centimetre, then I rushed upstairs and grabbed my lemonade. As I came back down to the hall, Grandma Sorrell was also just coming into it from the sitting room, or lounge, as she called it.

"I'll make a pot of tea, I think," she said.

"Oh, that's all right, I'll make it for you," I quickly offered, which almost brought a smile to her face, along with the words, "That's … er … nice." Again I wondered fleetingly whether lurking somewhere underneath the layers of hardness and coldness, was a soft centre.

I made the tea as fast as I could with the smallest amount of water in the kettle so it would boil quickly. It only half filled the teapot but then there was only one of her to drink it.

As I carried the tray carefully through to the front hall, the back door slowly opened and there stood Leah. I'd obviously given her an enormous shock because she looked deathly pale and completely paralysed. She'd certainly shocked me. My hands were trembling. If I wasn't careful I'd drop the tray.

"Let me go first," I whispered. "When you hear the lounge door shut, go up. I'll be twenty minutes."

She managed to utter, "OK," and I thought, poor Leah. She's going through absolute hell just because I want her to stay the night to make it less boring for me. I felt suddenly very selfish.

Balancing the tray on one hand, I opened the sitting-room door with the other. Grandma Sorrell had set out the cards. As soon as I'd put the tray down I shut the door with a bit of a bang to alert Leah.

The next fifteen minutes were very boring except that I found it fairly amusing to notice how often Grandma Sorrell looked at her watch. She couldn't wait for me to go to bed. But then the unexpected happened. The phone rang.

Grandma Sorrell answered it and spoke very few words before handing it to me because it was Mum. It was lovely to hear her voice but I just wished I could talk in private to her. Although Grandma Sorrell seemed to be busying herself tidying up, I really wanted her to go out of the room.

"How are you getting on?" I asked Mum.

"We're fine, *bibiche*, but what about you? I theenk about you so much. Is *Grand-mère* behaving herself?" Mum gave a light laugh as she said this.

"Reasonably well," I answered carefully.

"Ees she leestening?" Mum asked.

"Yes."

"OK. I'll ask you zee questions. Does she feed you well?"

"Yes."

"Ees she streect about bedtime?"

"Yes, very." There was a pause, then Mum's voice went serious.

"Eet won't be for long, *bibiche* – maybe less than sree weeks."

I thought I ought say something to cheer Mum up a bit. "I'm probably going to spend the night at Leah's tomorrow – and Grandma Sorrell might let Leah stay here one night next week."

"That's good. I'm pleased," she said. "Your faazer sends hees love," she added. I wondered whether or not Dad really did send his love or whether Mum was just saying that to make me feel better.

"When will you phone next?" I asked her. "Or is there a number where I can phone you?"

"Not yet," she said, suddenly sounding rather distant, as though the line wasn't very good any more. "I'll phone you on Sunday."

"OK. Love to Dad."

"*A bientôt, bibiche.*"

"*A bientôt, maman.*"

I put the phone down and felt quite heavy-hearted. Why, oh why, hadn't we had the whole conversation in French? It never occurred to me until just at the end. Mum and I often spoke together in French. It would have seemed in no way unnatural, and I could have said anything I'd wanted without Grandma Sorrell being any the wiser. Thinking about it though, I probably would have still said I was perfectly happy even if I was speaking in French. I didn't want Mum to have to worry when she was so far away.

"Time for bed, Agnès." Her voice just behind me gave me a shock.

"Can I take the cards up with me? I like playing patience."

"Yes, all right, just for a few minutes."

"And can I get something to eat? I'm a bit hungry and thirsty."

"Be quick then."

Disappearing quickly before she remembered the history project, I went into the kitchen, where I grabbed cheese, bread, apples and more lemon-ade before rushing upstairs. "Only me," I said, going into our bedroom. Leah got up from her usual hiding-place, still looking rather pale. "I can't wait until I'm a proper visitor here," she said, with a shaky smile.

"And I can't wait until tomorrow, but now let's play cards and have a feast."

I told Leah about Mum's phone call, and realized that I'd not really found out anything about what Mum and Dad were doing. For example, I wondered briefly what exactly Mum did all day long while Dad was at meetings and things.

Leah's pale face didn't change much as we played cards, and in the end she confessed that she wasn't feeling all that well, so we decided to go to bed. Leah snuggled down and fell asleep in no time at all. She must have been feeling lousy. I had the sudden selfish thought that if she was ill I might not be able stay the night with her.

I read my book for a while, then I must have fallen asleep too because the next thing I knew I was woken by a noise from downstairs. When I looked back on that night, a few days later, I realized there was no way I could have been woken by a noise from downstairs because I couldn't possibly have heard anything from up in our bedroom with the door closed. So maybe it was just some amazing instinct which woke me.

I switched on the bedside light and looked at my watch. It was a quarter to two in the morning.

Chapter 5

I glanced at Leah. She was fast asleep, snuggled right up, and seemed to be hardly breathing. I had almost convinced myself that I must have imagined or dreamt the noise, or that it was just an ordinary creaking sound that any old house made from time to time, when I heard it again. It was only very faint but it was coming from downstairs.

There's someone down there, I thought... It's probably only Grandma Sorrell... Maybe she goes to bed very late... Quarter to two, don't be ridiculous, Andy! Maybe she got up for a drink... No, she had a teasmade in her room. I knew that because Mum had told me... Maybe ... what if ... there was a burglar down there! After all, it was full of valuables, this house.

Oh, no! It was happening again. The idea was beginning to take root, and an even worse one was following shortly behind, also embedding itself in my mind. 1) This was a burglar, and 2) it was up to me to go down there and investigate.

Heart beating faster than usual, I put on my dressing gown and crept out on to the landing, shutting the door silently behind me. It felt cold on the landing and I shivered with each step. When I put my ear to Grandma Sorrell's door I could clearly hear her deep breathing, like gentle snoring. I made myself go on.

Only two of the stairs creaked as far as I knew, and I managed to step on another part of each of those, so going downstairs I was totally silent. It became gradually clearer to me, though, that there was definitely someone down there and that it couldn't be Grandma Sorrell, unless I'd been very much mistaken about the snoring coming from her bedroom.

So what was I going to do – me, a little girl of thirteen – if there was an armed burglar about? I stood trembling, desperately trying to think. Maybe I ought to wake up Grandma Sorrell? No, that would mean going back upstairs and knocking on her door to get her to unlock it. There was no way I was going to do that because the knocking would alert the burglar, who would quickly make his escape.

On the other hand, isn't that what I wanted? To get the burglar to just go away as quickly as possible. Another thought was entering my head. I could capture the burglar and be a hero. No, Andy! Don't even consider it. You'll get hurt. Forget it.

But, of course, I couldn't forget it. I took a deep breath and began to tiptoe across the hall towards the sitting room. Someone was definitely in there. I could hear paper rustling. The burglar might be rifling through Grandma Sorrell's desk looking for something.

I screwed up one eye and looked through the crack in the hinge side of the door, which was ajar. The man was fairly tall and thickset. I couldn't say much more than that because he was leaning forwards, not looking into the desk, but in one of the cupboards of the sideboard.

His trousers were greeny grey and he was wearing a tatty sort of T-shirt. His feet looked as though they were bare. He must have taken his shoes off to move more quietly. I wondered fleetingly where he'd left them. Probably just outside.

Now would be a perfect moment, I told myself. I'd just creep up behind him and knock him over the head with something. No, I couldn't. I'd never ever done anything like that before. I might kill him. I'd no idea how much force it would take to kill someone. On the other hand, if I just made lots of noise and he ran away, he'd probably leave with his pockets bulging with Grandma Sorrell's jewellery. For all I knew she kept her bank cards in that cupboard, and he could take those too, while he was at it.

I swallowed hard and looked around me. There was nothing to hit him with. Good. That meant I couldn't hit him. Stop being pathetic, Andy. Go and get something. I made myself go into the back lobby, and it's a good job I did, because the next thing I knew, he was out of the lounge and heading towards the stairs.

Omigod! He was going to murder Grandma Sorrell in her bed! No, he couldn't, because she kept her door locked. My heart was really beating by now because I'd realized something awful. He wouldn't know which bedroom was Grandma Sorrell's. He'd just go into any old bedroom which wasn't locked. My heart in my mouth, I thought about him attacking poor Leah as she lay asleep. I had to do something – and fast!

I crept back up the stairs as quickly and noise-lessly as I could, and noticed immediately that the first door on the right, which had been locked, was just a fraction open. So he'd some-how found a way in there, had he?

It took all my courage to look through the crack. I couldn't see the man and I didn't dare open the door any further, but what I could see was the back of the door reflected in the mirror across the room. And there in the lock of the door was a key. I had to act quickly.

Without giving myself chance to change my mind I opened the door another couple of centimetres, put my hand round the door and pulled out the key. I reckon my heartbeat was even louder than the rattle that the key made as I removed it, but at least I now had the key in my hand. I closed the door as fast as I could, and with trembling fingers put the key in the lock and turned it.

"Hey! What are you doing!" the man called out sharply as he banged on the inside of the door. "What do you think you're doing? Who's there?"

I knocked loudly on Grandma Sorrell's door to wake her up and tell her what I'd managed to do, before the man broke the door down or something.

"What on earth's going on?" came Grandma Sorrell's voice, which sounded cross, not scared. But wait till she saw what I'd done. Then she'd thank me.

"Grandma Sorrell," I began breathlessly as she emerged from the bedroom, wearing a hairnet and a big winceyette peach-coloured nightie, "you've got a burglar. He was in the lounge, and then he somehow got into that room there…" I pointed, though it was perfectly obvious where the banging and shouting was coming from.

Grandma Sorrell's face was looking very pale and serious.

"Don't worry, I've locked him in," I reassured her. "Look!" And I triumphantly handed over the key. She examined the key as though it might conceal the burglar's identity, then very slowly, without a word, she put it in the lock and turned it.

"Grandma Sorrell! What are you doing? You'll let the burglar out. He may attack you!"

The door opened and the man looked rather sheepishly at Grandma Sorrell. She returned the look with a stern one of her own. Then they both looked at me. I knew there was something wrong, something *very* wrong. I'd made a horrendous mistake. This wasn't a burglar. I'd no idea who it was, but it wasn't an intruder of any sort.

"This is Mr Coletram, Agnès. He's a guest."

Mr Coletram stuck his hand out, and I shook it, feeling absolutely stupid.

"Brave girl, brave girl," he said, pumping my hand and giving me an encouraging sort of half-smile. "Quite right, quite right. It could have been a burglar and you would have very skilfully caught him." He was still pumping my hand. I tried to let go but couldn't. "Gave me a bit of a shock, you know. I wondered what was happening when the key disappeared!"

At this point, thank goodness, he let go of my

hand. I didn't know what to say, I felt so pathetic, but worse than that I felt a huge sense of anti-climax. This was supposed to be my great moment of glory, and here I was barely escaping a telling-off if the look on Grandma Sorrell's face was anything to go by.

"I think you'd better go back to bed, Agnès," she informed me rather icily. So off I meekly went, though I didn't feel at all tired because my mind was working away. Mr Coletram might be a guest, but what on earth was he doing prying into Grandma Sorrell's sideboard? The only reason I decided against bringing up this rather sticky point, was the fact that I couldn't bear to look a fool twice in one night. After all, there might have been some perfectly logical reason. I decided to approach the conversation carefully when Grandma Sorrell was on her own.

Leah hadn't moved a muscle and was still breathing very lightly. I touched her forehead and she felt quite hot. I wondered whether she was sickening for something. "Please be better in the morning, Leah," I said to the ceiling. "I couldn't bear another night in this awful place."

I got into bed and lay rigidly on my back, knowing it would take me ages to get to sleep because I felt angry, depressed and worried. Also my brain was working at three hundred revs a minute on how to get out of spending the rest of three weeks under this roof.

Perhaps Grandma Sorrell would be perfectly happy if I disappeared for good because then she could relax with her "guest". Huh! She'd gone to great pains to conceal him, hadn't she? She'd made me go to bed early. It was all falling into place now. He must be her new boyfriend or something. Ugh! How revolting! No, he couldn't be her boyfriend. For one thing he looked too young for her.

I lay there for ages trying to think what to do. It was so tempting to wake Leah up and talk it all through with her, but I knew she needed her sleep. If she slept well there was more chance that she'd be better in the morning.

And then another thought occurred to me. I would phone Mami in France. Yes! Brilliant idea! She would be able to tell me what I ought to do. She'd probably heard from Mum and Dad anyway. Mum was very close to her mother and so was I. The French side of our family was all close. I looked at my watch. It said four-fifty. That meant it would have been five-fifty in France. That was still a bit early. I'd leave it half an hour then I would ring her. Mami and Papi were early risers so they'd definitely be awake.

With any luck Grandma Sorrell and Mr Coletram wouldn't get up before seven, especially as they'd been disturbed during the night. I'd be able to talk perfectly privately to Mami and Papi. So I lay back feeling a bit calmer, and read my book, then on the dot of five-thirty I crept down-stairs and went into the lounge, shutting the door behind me.

I dialled Mami's number and listened to the familiar French ring. In France it doesn't ring in twos like it does in England, just in a series of long single rings. After four of these the phone was picked up.

"'Allo," said a rather sleepy voice and I realized with a shock it was Mum! I thought I must have been dreaming or something. What was she doing there?

Then I got another shock because the lounge door was very slowly opening. I guiltily replaced the receiver and just stared wide-eyed at the door. Then I nearly fell over with relief because there, looking bleary-eyed and confused, was Leah.

"Are you OK?" I asked her gently.

"I woke up and wondered where you were, because you weren't in the loo," she replied. She was shivering.

"Let's get back up to bed before anyone catches us, and I'll tell you all about it," I whispered.

"All about what?"

"All about what's been happening while you've been fast asleep."

So we got back in the bed to keep warm and I

recounted the events of the night to an incredulous Leah, who couldn't stop gasping as my story unfolded.

"Wait till the others hear about this," she said two or three times. Then when I got to the end of the tale she said, "Your mum! But why don't you go back down and phone her again? It's still too early for Grandma Sorrell or that man to wake up."

"Because I don't want Mum to worry about me while she's away."

"But she's not away, she's with *her* mum. And you ought to be with *your* mum too!" Leah answered indignantly.

"Yes, you're right," I finally agreed, and I was about to go downstairs for the third time that night when there was a knock at my door, followed by Grandma Sorrell's rather harsh tones.

"Why are you talking, Agnès? You're not doing your history project *now*, I presume?"

"I'm talking to Herman, my gorilla," I answered quickly, as Leah dived under the bedclothes and made herself as flat as possible. "I do that sometimes when I'm trying to get back to sleep."

There was a grunt in answer from Grandma Sorrell, then I heard the faint slush of her disappearing slippered footsteps. From then on,

Leah and I spoke only in the softest of whispers. At least she was feeling better. That was one good thing. About the only good thing, I thought as I stared at the ceiling and wished away another few hours so I could get out of Bleak House at least until the next day.

The following afternoon we were all in the café. Five of us sat round a table with drinks, and Luce was working. Leah and I had been entertaining the others with tales of our action-packed evening and night. Luce kept finding things to do near our table, like watering the plants and sweeping up bits of non-existent dirt by our feet. This was all so that she could listen to our story. After a bit Jan appeared.

"What's this, a mothers' meeting?" she asked with a grin. "Come on Lucy, I'm sure you can catch up on the gossip later. There's a lot of work piling up in the kitchen." Luce sighed and went off to face the washing-up or whatever.

"I'll fill you in, don't worry," Jaimini called after her.

"So Grandma Sorrell's got a boyfriend, has she?" Fen asked with a giggle.

"I can't imagine anyone wanting to be Grandma Sorrell's boyfriend," I answered with considerable feeling.

"But if he was a perfectly innocent male guest,

why should she have to wait until you were safely tucked up in bed before letting him in?" Tash asked.

"Perhaps she didn't wait," Leah said. "Maybe he just happened to turn up."

"So what happened at breakfast time?" Jaimini wanted to know. "Did she introduce him?"

"I didn't see him again," I answered. "He was probably too embarrassed to show his face. He stayed in his room. 'Mr Coletram is having breakfast in his room,' Grandma Sorrell announced rather haughtily," I added with a laugh. Leah smiled but it seemed rather an effort.

"Are you OK?" I asked her, feeling concerned.

"Yes, honestly, I'm fine."

"Was it difficult to get your grandma to agree to let you stay the night at Leah's?" Tash asked.

"The difficult bit was persuading Kim to be mum," Leah answered.

"Grandma Sorrell insisted on checking up that I wouldn't be gallivanting around, as she put it," I carried on with the tale, "so we got Kim to phone her pretending to be Pat, before Grandma Sorrell could phone Leah's house and speak to Pat personally."

"That would have been a disaster, wouldn't it?" commented Jaimini.

"You're not kidding! Imagine the consequences if Pat had said, 'Oh, and thank you so much for having Leah to stay last night, Mrs Sorrell!'"

We all laughed rather nervously at this thought, then I told them my orders. "She said to make sure I was back by five o'clock on Sunday evening at the very latest. She also wanted me to leave her Leah's phone number in case she needed to contact me in an emergency, though goodness knows what emergency could possibly arise where she needed me around…"

"Well, now she knows you're so skilful with burglars," Fen said, jokingly.

"I'm surprised she let you go at all," Jaimini commented thoughtfully.

"She did check up in the directory that the number I'd given her was really Leah's number," I said.

"I reckon she's too obsessed with her new boy-friend to worry about visiting granddaughters," Fen said lightly. "Did she warn you about not coming to the café?"

"Only about a hundred times," I answered sarcastically.

"Look!" Tash suddenly said, which made us all look round frantically.

"What?" asked Fen.

"Don't look now," Tash hissed.

"But you just said look," I pointed out.

"On table five," Tash whispered, leaning forwards confidentially. "It's that woman I was telling you about. She can't keep her eyes off this table."

Luce appeared at that moment and caught what Tash was saying. "What woman? What woman? Tell me," she said, desperate for a bit of gossip.

"Don't look now, but table five. That's the second time she's been in here on her own. Yesterday she was staring at me as though I was a pink flamingo."

"What other colours do flamingoes come in then?" Jaimini asked, jokingly.

"Well madam, we do a nice little blue one and a rather large fluffy purple one," Luce answered, turning into a saleswoman quick as a flash. We all laughed because she's such a great actress. By that time we'd had a chance to get a good look at the lady, who must have been aware of our interest because she suddenly took a magazine out of her bag and started studying it. "I'll ask Jan if she knows who she is," Luce said, heading off towards the kitchen. She returned a moment later and informed us that Jan said her name is Miss or Mrs Claw, and that she's either single or divorced.

"So why is she so interested in me?" Tash asked.

"Goodness only knows," Fen replied. "Oh, look!"

Again we all looked, and there coming through the door was little Marine with a woman who had to be her mother because she looked so much like Marine, or rather Marine looked so much like her. She must have been in her early thirties, quite attractive, but rather strained-looking. She was wearing jeans with a white T-shirt tucked into them. Her brown hair was tied back in a ponytail.

Marine was touching her mother's arm and pointing to me. She wasn't smiling – just pointing. Her mother smiled at us all, not knowing which one was me, so as soon as they'd sat down, I went over and sat with them. Jan came to take their order and I noticed that the mother spoke perfect English with no accent. But then when she spoke to Marine her French was just as perfect.

"Hi, I'm Andy," I said, "short for Agnès."

"I'm Sylvie," she said. "I'm really pleased to meet you. One of the mothers at Marine's school told me about you – you know that Marine seems to have taken to you."

"But didn't … didn't Marine tell you herself?"

"No…" She suddenly looked taken aback. "I'm sorry, I thought you knew that Marine isn't speaking…"

"You mean, she doesn't even speak at home? Not to you, even?"

Sylvie shook her head with a look of sad acceptance. I didn't say anything for a moment to see if she wanted to tell me more. My brain was doing overtime trying to work out why a perfectly healthy seven-year-old should choose not to speak. Sylvie wasn't offering any more for the moment, though. Perhaps she didn't want to say too much in front of Marine. I thought it best to turn my attention to Marine herself.

I grinned at her and said in English, "How have you been doing, Marine? I've missed you. I'm staying at my grandma's for a while, you see." Marine just looked at me. Her eyes didn't hold any expression at all. It was weird talking to someone when their shutters were completely down like that.

"Doesn't she understand English?" I asked Sylvie, trying to get to the bottom of this.

"Yes, she understands perfectly. I've brought her up to be bilingual like me."

"I thought you must be bilingual," I said. We grinned at each other, because it was quite rare, I suppose, to have three bilingual people sitting round the same table. "So why..." I began hesitantly. I didn't like talking about Marine as though she wasn't there, but there wasn't really any alternative because she wouldn't talk herself.

Sylvie shook her head. It was just a very small movement, but it told me not to ask why Marine wouldn't speak. I'd obviously hit a nerve which got me intrigued, but I quickly changed my question to, "So why do you like coming into this café so much, Marine?" Again she didn't answer. I wasn't really expecting her to.

I decided to try the same question in French because Sylvie had shrugged and gave me a look which seemed to say, "See, hopeless."

"*Ça te plaît bien, de venir au café, Marine?*" This time she nodded and the shutters went from her eyes. Good, I was really getting somewhere. She obviously felt more comfortable with French than with English. Every time I spoke to Marine after that it was in French. I wondered if I was allowed to ask Sylvie how long it was since Marine had last spoken, or whether this was also something that she wouldn't want to discuss in front of Marine. "Have you lived in England long?" I asked carefully.

"For ages," she answered. "It was in England that I met my husband, Marine's father. He's half French and half English too. It was such a co-incidence meeting him over here because we were students at the time, but it was the holidays and we were both travelling round and getting casual work along the way."

"So did you meet at work?"

"We met in a pub where I was already working, and Tom had come to apply for a job. When we got chatting we realized that we both came from the same part of France and both had French fathers and English mothers. We hit it off immediately and got married as soon as we'd both finished as students."

"So Marine has lived all her life in England?" I asked.

Sylvie nodded and smiled, then glanced over at Leah and the others. "I don't want to keep you from your friends," she said, looking concerned, "but I wondered if you'd like to come back to our place one day? I know Marine would like that."

Marine gave me another of her nearly smiles, so I knew that she must be keen, as that was her very strongest communication. I was keen too, because 1) it would be another escape route from Grandma Sorrell and 2) I was curious to talk to Sylvie when Marine wasn't around, so I could find out more about why she was refusing to speak. There'd be more chance of that at her home than here, all stuck round a table.

"I'd love to come," I said happily. "I'll have to check with my grandma though. She's very strict," I added, wrinkling my nose at Sylvie, who wrinkled her nose too, which told me straight away that she sympathized with me for having to stay with a strict grandmother.

"Perhaps if I had a word with her?"

"That would be brilliant," I agreed, so we left

it that Sylvie would phone in the next two or three days.

I'd hardly sat back down at our table when, for the third time, I heard the word, "Look!" This time it was Leah who had spoken. I craned round again to see that Mandy was making her way very cautiously into the café.

As her eyes, slowly scanning the café, met mine, I gave her an encouraging smile and she lit up straight away and came over to our table.

"I was looking to see if any of my friends from school are here, because they sometimes are on Saturday afternoons."

Poor Mandy. She seemed so alone. She'd already told me that she was the only one of her group of friends who lived so far out of Cableden.

I grabbed a chair from another table and she sat in our circle, looking pleased to be welcomed by a load of year eights, because very often the year eights despise the year sevens, only *we* aren't like that.

"Did you come here on the bus?" Leah asked conversationally.

"Yes. Mum's working again today," Mandy answered, sounding fed up, but trying not to show it.

"What's your mum's job?" Tash asked.

"She works behind the bar in a pub," Mandy replied. "She was there till late last night as well."

"Have you got any brothers or sisters?" Jaimini asked.

"No."

"Me neither," Jaimini quickly responded which seemed to cheer Mandy up.

"I haven't got a dad either," Mandy went on. None of us knew what to say when she said that, but she quickly went on to explain that her parents were divorced, and her dad had moved a long way away so she hadn't seen him for years.

"My parents are divorced too," Tash put in quickly. "And I live with just Mum too."

Again Mandy shot a grateful look, this time to Tash. It made me think how nice my friends were, trying to make Mandy feel normal, but now we were a bit stuck for conversation. Mandy seemed to be looking round nervously. I gave her a questioning look.

"I keep wondering if those boys are going to come in – Darren and the others," she explained.

"Why?" Leah and I asked together.

"Because they sometimes follow me around, especially on Saturdays. They get a buzz out of doing it. It's really awful because they're always on about Mum."

"But she's really good-looking, your mum is," said Leah, sounding full of indignation on Mandy's behalf.

"I know she is. She's almost too perfect,"

Mandy answered with another sigh. Mandy herself had the same lovely skin as her mother, and although she also had nice features, she was a bit plump and her hair was in a style that didn't really suit her. I could see why the boys mocked her. It wasn't just because of her mum. It was because she was a good target, always on her own, and also because she didn't look cool enough. Typical of horrible boys like that.

That's why they had a go at me, because I'm so small. I didn't think they'd waste their time on me any more though, because it wasn't so much fun if the person you were jeering or sneering at couldn't care less. Darren and the others got much more of a kick out of taunting Mandy because it made her so upset and uncomfortable every time. Nasty boys! I'd like to sink my teeth into Darren Kirk's arm and make him really yell!

As if on cue, he strolled into the café, with his usual two mates in tow.

Chapter 6

The sight of Darren like that gave me an instant flashback to when Gary Barker was in here, because it was the same two friends with a new leader. Mandy seemed to go rigid with terror. The others leaned forward and started talking like mad because they didn't want anything to do with Darren. But I didn't join in. I stayed sitting in exactly the same position, feeling really mad that we had to be dictated to by such a dingbat.

"Don't let him see you," Mandy whispered, tugging urgently at my sweatshirt to bring me into their tight little circle.

"He's sure to see me, Mandy," I said patiently. "You've got to stand up to him, then he'll stop riling you."

At that moment my eye caught the eye of the woman who had been staring earlier on. Again she quickly looked back to her magazine, but it couldn't have just been coincidence that she found our table so interesting.

Then Marine and Sylvie got up to go.

"Salut Marine, à bientôt, hein?"

The moment they were out of the door I heard Darren's voice imitating me, but in a far more high-pitched babyish tone. "Saloo Marine. A biantow." His accent was really bad. Any French person would have had a job understanding what he was saying.

"That's one GCSE you may as well say good-bye to, Darren," I called casually and not very loudly. I didn't want Jan coming over here and telling me to pipe down. On the other hand I wasn't going to put up with *anything* from Darren Kirk.

"Shut up, Andy," hissed Leah, also trying to draw me into their huddle.

Luce was standing at Darren's table, note pad at the ready to take the orders. Of course, they wouldn't know that she was one of our group of friends, or even that she was year eight. She looked totally confident standing there so they didn't start mocking her.

"Coke," I heard Darren say rather rudely. The others both then said the same thing.

"Three Cokes," Luce repeated, as she turned to go.

Darren couldn't resist it. "Oh great, she can count up to three," he said, grinning at the others who sniggered dutifully at their leader's great joke. I could tell they wished Darren would shut up, though. In fact, one of them leaned forward and started talking earnestly to Darren. His eyes kept flicking over in our direction so it was obvious he was talking about us. Maybe he was warning him about the downfall of their old hero, Gary Barker, who had been exactly the same sort of horrible bully as Darren was, but we'd managed to get one over on him and made him look a complete fool. It had been absolutely brilliant.

From where she was standing at the counter, doing the Cokes, Luce had caught my eye. She had given me the faintest of raised eyebrows as if to say, "Is this that nasty boy from the bus?" and I had given her a barely detectable nod. So now Luce was making her way back to Darren's table carrying two Cokes on her tray. She put them down on his table, one in front of each of his mates, then she started to walk away.

Good old Luce, I thought. She'd obviously heard what he'd said about being able to count, and decided to pay him back. She'd got guts, Luce had, and it was all done without her saying a single word, so far.

"Oy! Where's mine then?"

Luce turned round and looked innocently at the two Cokes, then pointing slowly to each one she said, "One … two."

"We ordered three," Darren said indignantly.

"Oh, so you did, it's just that I'm not very good at counting," Luce said with a sarcastic smile. "I'll go and get you another one, but it might be quite a while, because I haven't got a very good memory either."

"Bravo, serves him right," two young women at the next table said, casting a disgusted look at Darren, who actually went red. Then Luce came over to us and crouched down beside me. We introduced Mandy who simply stared in awe at Luce.

"Well done," I told her warmly. "That's the only way to handle them."

"I wished I dared to talk like that to them," Mandy sighed.

"You will by the time we've finished with you," said Luce with a wink. "I'd better get back to work."

I got up to go to the loo, and had to walk past the boys' table.

"She your friend, then?" Darren asked, jerking his head in Luce's direction.

"Yes, she is," I answered simply.

"Tell her if she don't bring me that Coke straight away, you're for it on Monday."

"I'm not telling her anything," I retorted calmly. "She's just doing her job and I wouldn't dream of interfering."

"Right, you just wait," he said, ominously quietly, through clenched teeth.

When I came back from the loo Luce was only just delivering the Coke and I could see that Darren was really seething. She put it down calmly and he didn't say anything.

"Oh, no," wailed Leah softly.

"What!"

"Darren's eyes are positively boring into you, and he looks mad as anything."

"Let me worry about that," I reassured her.

Shortly afterwards we all said goodbye to Luce, then went. I had to admit it was quite disturbing that Darren had gone so quiet. His anger was obviously smouldering away, and I found that much more difficult to deal with than the fronty jeers and taunts.

As we walked off I glanced in quickly through the café window, to see the nosey woman get up to go. It occurred to me that she might be a spy or something, but I quickly forgot about her.

Leah and I went happily off to her house, hiring a video on the way. Pat and Stuart, Leah's mum and dad, were both out in their little garden when we got back, but Stuart immediately came in and asked me if I wanted a quick game of draughts. So Leah made everyone a cup of tea, and there was lovely homemade carrot cake on the tray when she came back from the kitchen.

"Courtesy of Kim," she said, slicing it lovely and thickly.

"Where is Kim anyway?" I asked.

"Gadding about somewhere," Pat said, coming in and shaking her head with a bit of tut-tutting, as though she'd lost all control of her older daughter.

"She's only out with Danny, Mum," Leah pointed out, mildly. Danny, by the way, is Tash's brother. He's a little bit older than Kim and really good-looking.

"Hmm, out with Danny, eh?" said Stuart, absent-mindedly puffing on his pipe. He's always like that, Stuart is. He never really joins in conversations, just adds extra bits to them. Pat gets exasperated with him sometimes, but Leah loves him being like that, and I thought how sweet and nice he was.

By Sunday morning it was obvious Leah wasn't well. She had a temperature and she just didn't feel like getting out of bed.

"I'm sorry, Andy," she kept saying, "but you don't have to go back. You can stay here with Mum and Dad. They won't mind." Kim was there too, and she assured me that it would be fine to stay, but I felt guilty when Leah was stuck up in bed.

"Look, just stay here and have lunch with us then," Pat said.

"Then we can have a game of chess if you want," Stuart added, eyes twinkling under his rather bushy eyebrows, pipe puffing.

"OK. I'll stay. Thank you very much." So Stuart and I played chess and he won, but only just.

"You're the best opponent I've had for a long time," he told me, patting me on the back. "I don't get *any* opponents in this house. Can't you teach Leah how to play? She won't listen to her old dad," he said, jokingly.

At about four o'clock, Stuart said he'd run me back to Grandma Sorrell's. I couldn't say "Bye" to Leah because she was fast asleep. We didn't talk much on the journey, but it was a nice companionable silence. I was beginning to feel depressed though, at the thought of Bleak House and boredom.

"Be glad when your parents are back, I guess?" Stuart suddenly said, obviously sensing my mood.

"Yeah," I admitted with a light laugh. "Grandma Sorrell certainly isn't the most easy-going person in the entire world."

"Come and stay with us again in a few days," Stuart said.

"I'd love to, but I'm not sure she'll let me during the week. She might let Leah come over again though," I added thoughtfully as we pulled up outside Bleak House.

"Thanks very much for the lift, Stuart," I said as I heaved my bag out of the back seat.

"I'll just wait here till I see you're safely in," Stuart smiled back.

I went round to the back door and it was locked, so I walked round to the patio doors and they were slightly open. What I saw in the sitting room gave me quite a shock.

There was Grandma sitting rather rigidly on the settee, and beside her, sat Mr Coletram with – get this! – his arm round Grandma Sorrell! My eyes nearly popped out of my head. In fact, I don't know how they managed to stay in their sockets.

"My granddaughter will be back any time now, Leslie," Grandma Sorrell said, and it was at that moment that Mr Coletram spotted me standing there open-mouthed.

"Hello ... er, Andy," he said, removing his arm. He didn't look all that embarrassed, though. Grandma Sorrell, on the other hand, shot into the air and said, "How long have you been standing there? Why didn't you say something?"

"I only just got here," I managed to utter. Though the truthful answer would have been,

"The reason I didn't say anything was because my mouth was stuck in an open position."

"Come in then, child. Don't just stand there."

"I'll just say bye to Leah's dad," I gabbled, and quickly ran back to the car to give Stuart a nod and a wave, before walking slowly back to the romantic couple.

Well, what a turn up for the books! So this was the "Lesley" that Grandma Sorrell had mistaken me for, when I'd phoned the other day. It had never entered my head that Lesley could be a man.

Grandma Sorrell had obviously been trying to compose herself during my brief absence. "Mr Coletram is a close friend, Agnès," she began rather formally, "so naturally you may see quite a bit of him during your stay here."

I nodded and tried for a smile.

"Don't be so high and mighty, Joan," Mr Coletram said, putting his arm round Grandma Sorrell's shoulder again, which made her go stiff as a ramrod. "Your grandmother and I are more than close friends," he said to me, "we're…"

I waited, wondering which word he was going to choose. None of them would be right: "Boyfriend and girlfriend!" "Going out with each other!" I could feel a giggle coming to the surface. Please God, don't let me laugh when he says it, I said rapidly to myself over and over again.

"We're … going to be married," he said finally. My giggle immediately sank and fizzled out because this was serious stuff. Grandma Sorrell (Joan!) was looking a mixture of stern and confused. It occurred to me that perhaps Mr Coletram hadn't actually asked her to marry him yet.

"Congratulations, that's great. I'm really pleased," I said. And it was true. If Mr Coletram could turn Grandma Sorrell into a softer, nicer person, I might even finish up quite liking her. Stranger things than that had happened!

The next day at morning break I was bursting with my news. I broke it to the others in our usual meeting place at the bottom of the netball courts. Only Leah wasn't there, because she was off school, so presumably still ill. I wondered what it was she'd got, and also wished I could see her. The others thought my news was wonderful.

"Fancy Grandma Sorrell having a secret boyfriend!" said Luce. "I can't imagine what on earth he sees in her."

"Me neither," Jaimini agreed. "I've only seen your grandmother once before, Andy, but she looked far too strict and straight to have any men friends."

"Well, she did have a husband once," I reminded them. "My grandfather. He was a nice old man. He was smaller than her, quite a bit smaller actually, and I always remember his little finger curled right over because of his arthritis. He was always chuckling to himself. I used to visit him a lot..."

"How long ago was that?" Tash asked me.

"Ages. Nearly six years. He used to take me for long walks to interesting places. I wish he was still alive."

"Maybe that's why your grandmother seems to be such a hard woman now," Fen suggested.

"Yes, I think you're right," I agreed. "She never used to be like she is now. Mum says she put up that tough suit of armour to protect herself from her emotions."

"And now the armour's started to get chinks in it," Luce finished off, taking us back to where we had started.

"Hmm," I said thoughtfully. "Well, let's hope there are enough chinks so that she doesn't mind if I phone and tell her I'm going to be late after school. I want to go and see Leah just to check she's not got anything seriously the matter with her."

"What about the café? It's Leah's turn, isn't it?" Tash said, looking worried, but Fen said she would do it for her.

"What about my turn tomorrow?" I hardly dared ask.

"I'll do it, don't worry," Tash quickly offered.

"I'll phone Grandma Sorrell, I think," I said decisively, "and ask if I'm allowed to go and see Leah after school. If she reacts fairly reasonably to that, I'll risk working at the café tomorrow."

"What, you mean you're going to tell the truth?" Jaimini asked.

"No, that would be taking it a bit far. I'll say I've got a sports practice, I think."

"But what about the bus? There isn't one after six o'clock, is there?"

I frowned. Jaimini was right. I was stuck.

"Don't worry, I can do it," Tash repeated her offer. "And maybe your mum and dad'll be back by next week."

"Have you heard from your mum again?" Jaimini asked.

"Grandma Sorrell said she phoned on Sunday and I was out. If she doesn't phone again, I'm going to phone her."

"Have you got her number?"

"No, but I'm going to phone her at my French grandparents."

"Maybe she was only visiting them, that last time when you phoned."

"It's a funny thing to do in the middle of a business trip," I said, thoughtfully. "I'd like to talk to Mami and Papi anyway, even if Mum isn't there."

I waited till lunchtime, then went to phone Grandma Sorrell. "Hello, Grandma Sorrell, it's Andy here."

"Yes?"

Uh-oh. She sounded as though she was in a particularly bad mood. "Leah's not at school today and I'd like to go and visit her after school. Is it all right if I come home on the five o'clock bus?"

"It's not a good idea, visiting ill people, Andy. I don't want you catching whatever Leah's got."

"Oh, I'll keep well away from her. Don't worry."

"Hmm."

There was a silence and I wasn't sure if I should break it. In the end, I had to break it before my money ran out.

"So can I?"

"I want you back at five-thirty and not a second later. And that's just this once, mind. Don't think I'm going soft just because ... well, don't think I'm going soft."

She was going to say, "...just because I've got a man around," I'm sure.

"OK, Grandma Sorrell. Thanks very much. See you later."

I put the phone down and scowled. "That bad, eh?" Fen joked.

"Awful," I agreed briefly.

After school I was just going out of the school gates when Mandy caught me up.

"I was waiting by the year-eight door for you," she said, sounding a bit hurt.

"Oh, sorry Mandy. I came out of the main exit today. I'm going to see Leah. She's not well." Mandy's expression turned to one of horror, and I immediately started worrying about her travelling on the bus on her own.

"Will you be OK?" I asked, but something told me she wouldn't. That morning on the bus, Darren hadn't said a word to either of us. Nor had he done any sniggering with his friends. I'd glanced at him twice and each time I'd found his eyes already on me. The look in them was quite frightening. He can't harm me while I'm on a bus, I'd kept telling myself, and that's what I said to Mandy now.

"He can't harm you while you're on the bus, you know, and your mum'll be there when you get off, won't she?"

"She usually is," Mandy mumbled in agreement, but I could tell she was feeling really fed up because I wasn't going to be there to stick up for her.

"Maybe it'll be Mrs Payne," I said to try and cheer her up.

Mandy nodded and tried to force a smile.

"I'll tell you what, when I've been to see Leah,

I'll nip back to my grandma's, do my homework, then ask if I can go for a walk, and I'll come to your house, OK?"

"Yeah, that'd be great," Mandy said, looking a little less downcast.

"Good luck," I added as we parted.

I thought about her all the way to Leah's because it wasn't fair that she had to go through this fear twice a day. I made a resolution to try and do something positive to help her, but I wasn't sure what.

Leah was downstairs watching TV when I turned up at her place. She was really pleased to see me, and couldn't believe the news about Grandma Sorrell and Leslie Coletram.

"I'll be back at school tomorrow," she told me. "Fen phoned me to say she's doing my duty at the café. I'm doing hers on Thursday."

"I'm thinking of risking doing mine tomorrow," I told Leah and she gasped at my daring, or foolhardiness. "What if you get found out?"

"I'm going to say I've got a sports meeting. Will you be at the café?"

"No, it's my piano lesson tomorrow."

I ran all the way to the bus stop because the last thing I wanted was to be late and miss the bus. As it happened I had another five minutes to wait. This was an ordinary bus, not a special school one. It felt completely different from the school bus – much nicer. I got off at my stop and walked quickly towards Bleak House thinking that at least Grandma Sorrell wouldn't be able to complain that I was late.

Deep in thought, wondering how Mandy had got on, I jumped at the sound of a voice behind me.

"Wanna see your friend?"

It was Darren. He sounded at his most menacing, and as I turned to face him I knew immediately that trouble was brewing.

"What friend?" I asked, matching his tone of voice to show that he didn't scare me, because at that moment I had only just started to feel anxious.

"Barbie Doll's daughter," he answered, cruelly.

"I'm seeing Mandy later," I told him coldly, then I turned abruptly and walked briskly on.

"No, you ain't, because she ain't at home," Darren told me, which made me stop in my tracks. I felt a surge of anger sweep through my body.

"What have you done to her?" I asked, turning on him and trembling with fury.

He grinned and didn't say a word. I knew he was enjoying my anger, but there was nothing I could do about that. I was furious and getting really worried.

"Wanna see her?"

I looked at my watch and thought fast. If I went

back to Grandma Sorrell's, I'd be making poor Mandy suffer for even longer. On the other hand, if I didn't report back to Grandma Sorrell I'd have hell to pay, and she probably wouldn't let me go to my "sports meeting" after school the following day.

"Where is she, then?" I snapped at the still grinning Darren.

"I'll show you," was all he would say.

I only hesitated for a second. "Make it fast," I retorted coldly.

Of course, he didn't. He just strolled along, turning down this little cutting. I followed him feeling a mixture of frustration, hate, anger and fear. My heart was beating faster with every step because despite all that our teachers and my parents had drummed into me, here I was going off to a lonely place with Darren.

I knew it was a stupid thing to do, but I also knew that if he'd somehow managed to harm Mandy, I'd never forgive myself if I didn't go and help her.

"How much further?" I snapped at Darren when nearly five minutes had gone by. We were walking across a field towards some derelict out-houses that used to belong to one of the big houses at the back of Grandma Sorrell's place, but weren't used for anything now, as far as I knew. My heart missed a beat because I suddenly knew where I was going to find Mandy.

"She'd better not be in here," I said, through gritted teeth, as Darren unbarred the door of the smallest, most ramshackle-looking shed.

"See for yourself."

I peered into the gloom and the next thing I knew, he'd shoved me hard in the back and I fell forward on to my knees into the semi–darkness, dragging my school bag behind me. He kicked my bag and slammed shut the door, so I was plunged into blackness.

I heard the bar bang into place on the other side of the door at the same time as I heard Mandy's terrified voice come out of the dark.

"Andy, thank God."

Chapter 7

Mandy couldn't say any more because she was crying. I yelled something through the door to Darren that's not repeatable, but I doubt he heard it because there was not a sound from outside, and I guessed he'd already legged it before anyone caught him red-handed.

"What are we going to do?" wailed Mandy. "My mum will be out of her mind with worry."

"And my grandmother won't exactly be over the moon, either," I mumbled grimly. What a stupid situation to be in. How could I have been so foolish as to walk straight into his trap? I kicked the wall angrily.

"What's that?" Mandy asked, because we could hardly see each other.

"Only me kicking this stupid shed," I answered, then my eyes began to get accustomed to the dark and I could more or less make out the sad, slumped form of Mandy in the corner. I felt really sorry for her. She must have been absolutely terrified to be left like this on her own for well over an hour, without even knowing whether anyone was going to turn up.

I crouched down beside her and put my arm round her. "Don't worry, we'll get out of here somehow," I told her, hoping my anger made me sound confident, because as each second went by I was becoming more and more afraid that we wouldn't.

"But how?" Mandy asked. "Nobody passes by here and Darren's made sure we're shut in. I tapped all over one wall and felt no rotten wood or anything, just some sort of deep scratches low down."

"I wonder what this is?" I said to myself, as I ran my hands over the nearest wall.

"It might be the scratches I found. Like someone's carved some writing into the wood."

"Well, that won't help us to get out. Let me feel the other walls," I went on briskly. So I started on the back wall and again, nothing magically gave way. On the third wall, though, my hands ran over something upraised and rough.

"Hang on a sec," I said, feeling the teeniest bit excited at my discovery. "There must be a window behind here. Someone's boarded it up from the inside for some reason."

"Can we get the board off?" Mandy asked, getting up and groping her way over to help me. We tried to get our fingers behind it, but it was no good. It was firmly nailed in place and it would not budge. Then I remembered my school bag. I found my ruler and tried to prise off the board with that, but all I succeeded in doing was break-ing the ruler.

"It's no good," I said finally, heaving a big sigh of disappointment which quickly turned back into anger.

In my fury I kicked the door really hard, and then froze because there was a loud thump from outside. Cautiously, I pressed against the door, and miracle of miracles, it opened! My enormous kick must have dislodged the bar.

"Right, we're out of here," I said, grabbing Mandy by the arm. She looked awful. Her face was all blotchy.

"What if he's waiting in hiding somewhere?" she said, through gritted teeth.

"I'll kill him, that's what," I answered grimly. She was still hanging back for some reason or other. "Come on, Mandy," I urged her.

"I just want to see what that carving in the wall is," she said.

My curiosity got the better of me, too, and I stood at the door holding it wide open to let in as much light as possible while Mandy tried to decipher the writing. She started to slowly speak the words she was reading.

"Da … rren … I … am … shut … in…"

We looked at each other and didn't say anything for a moment, then we set off for Mandy's place, concentrating only on getting there as quickly as possible. "I'll come back to your place with you. I'm already so late for Grandma Sorrell that another fifteen minutes won't make any difference."

"When do you think he wrote that?" Mandy suddenly asked, which proved that like me she'd been thinking about the words carved into the wood too.

"He must have been shut in there at some time or another – maybe when he was a little boy."

We didn't say any more about it after that because I suppose, like me, Mandy must have felt her emotions all mixed up. It was hard to be quite so angry when you realized that Darren had probably suffered the same fate as us, but been much more terrified.

"Where ever have you been?" asked Mandy's mum as she hugged Mandy tight. "I've been worried sick. Nobody's hurt you, have they?"

Mandy broke free and assured her mum she was all right. Then between the two of us we explained all that had happened. As we told our

120

story, I watched Mandy's mum's expression change from horror to anger, then to something softer – I'm not sure what, resignation, maybe.

"If only I'd been there at the bus stop … I had to stay on at work an extra half-hour today, we were so busy…"

"Are you going to report Darren to the Head, Mum?"

"He certainly deserves to be punished… I'll give it some thought."

"Are you going to tell his mum of him?"

"His … mother's got a lot on her plate…"

I couldn't understand why her temper had suddenly dissolved.

"Mum and Darren's mum both work at the same place," Mandy explained to me.

I could see that that would make it awkward, of course, but I still didn't understand why Mandy's mum had done such a complete turn-around as soon as she knew that Darren was responsible. "I'd better be going," I said. "I've got the worst ordeal to come," I added softly.

Mandy filled her mum in on my situation and her mum offered to talk to Grandma Sorrell if I thought that would help.

"Don't worry," I told her, probably sounding much more confident than I felt. "She'll be all right once she realizes there was nothing I could do about it."

Mandy's mum nodded, and then thanked me very much for rescuing her daughter, adding, "You must come again and stay for tea next time. Mandy's so much happier now you're around. My name's Lara, by the way."

On the way back to Grandma Sorrell's I started composing my opening lines in my head. I didn't want her flying at me in a big temper. I prayed that Mr Coletram would be there because he'd probably make her see reason. My prayer was answered. The back door was open so I went in and found them in the sitting room. Grandma Sorrell looked as though she was going to burst with anger.

"It wasn't my fault," I gabbled. "There's this really nasty boy on the bus and he told me he'd got my friend Mandy. He said he'd show me where she was and so I had to follow him, because Mandy could have been in great danger. And when we got there, he shoved me in too, and barred the door so we couldn't get out. Mandy was really terrified."

Grandma Sorrell's expression hadn't changed one iota while I'd been giving my excuse, and even when I suddenly paused for breath she didn't say anything. Mr Coletram looked concerned, but much more interested in how Grandma Sorrell was going to react. He studied her face and waited for her to speak.

"I've never heard such a load of nonsense in my entire life," she said finally, staring at me coldly. "If you're going to make up excuses, Agnès, at least make them sound vaguely plausible. Go upstairs and do your homework. And you can forget about having friends over as well. You're obviously not to be trusted."

"Wait a minute, Joan…" began Mr Coletram, who obviously thought Grandma Sorrell was being too hard on me.

"No, I won't wait a minute," she snapped at him. "I've waited enough minutes," she added with a glare at me.

I don't fly off the handle very easily, but I won't be spoken to like that when I don't deserve it. I faced Grandma Sorrell with a set expression, raised my chin and said, "You're being totally unreasonable. I've told you nothing but the truth. You can check out my story with Mandy's mother if you want."

That took the wind out of her sails. She looked rather confused all of a sudden but tried not to show it by speaking in her cross voice. Only now, because I'd thrown her off balance, it came out sounding gruff and odd.

"I don't even know this Mandy person, so I'm not likely to speak to her mother, am I? I suppose that's what you're relying on?"

Remembering suddenly Lara's rapid change of

reaction I decided it probably wouldn't be wise for Grandma Sorrell to speak to her. "The number's in the telephone directory. It's up to you," I said, hoping that this would make her believe me without needing to confirm it by phoning.

"You must have provoked him in some way. Boys don't do things like that for no reason," she persisted.

"The only thing I did was stick up for Mandy because he said nasty things about her mother," I replied.

"Well, you're back now," she said, sounding like a judge summing up in a court case.

"Safe and sound," Mr Coletram added, as though he thought *someone* should at least appear to be happy to see me.

"That's right," Grandma Sorrell managed to mutter, which was the nearest she ever got to showing she actually cared about me, I suppose. I announced that I was going to do my homework and she told me that tea would be in twenty minutes. As I mounted the stairs I wondered how on earth I was going to put my mind to geography when it was all crammed up with Darren Kirk.

At teatime in the dining room, Mr Coletram and Grandma Sorrell did most of the talking and I left them to it, because I didn't feel like talking to a nasty old bag who couldn't even apologize for misjudging me. There was one thing I wanted to know, though.

"Has Mum phoned?"

"Not yet."

Good. That meant that I'd get to talk to her. The trouble was, I was desperate to talk in private. Then I remembered. Of course, I could speak in French.

Mr Coletram had made a lovely big fruit salad and there was a jug of very inviting-looking thick cream in the middle of the table. I really enjoyed that bit of the meal. As I was eating I watched Mr Coletram watching Grandma Sorrell. At first I thought he was looking for a reaction to his fruit salad, and sure enough, after a few moments Grandma Sorrell managed a compliment – a rare thing.

"Very nice fruit salad…" She gave him a quick sidelong smile.

"Well, thank you, Joan," he replied. Even after that though, he kept his eyes on her a lot of the time.

This must be true love, I thought. Yet, it wasn't right somehow. How could anyone in their right mind be in love with Grandma Sorrell? She'd built such a strong shell around her since Grandpa's death it seemed completely impenetrable.

Maybe she takes off the shell when she's alone with Mr Coletram, I thought. Suddenly I couldn't bear the silence any more. I decided to furnish them with more details of Mandy's and my imprisonment. Grandma Sorrell tried not to show too much interest in this, but I'd actually got her gripped.

Mr Coletram simply wasn't interested. That was perfectly obvious. His eyes had stopped studying Grandma Sorrell and he was casting glances round the room. Why did I find him so shifty? I didn't know what it was, but there was definitely something disconcerting about Leslie Coletram.

The conversation moved on to the next day and Grandma Sorrell wanted to know what lessons I had at school. I made a big thing of the PE lesson, and told her enthusiastically how PE was my very favourite subject. She practically snorted with disgust when I said that, which brought Mr Coletram's eyes back on to her for a brief moment before they went roaming off round the room again.

When I was right in the middle of sowing seeds about the athletics meeting after school the following day, Mr Coletram got up and said he was going outside for a smoke.

"I didn't know Mr Coletram smoked?" I commented as soon as he'd gone.

"Disgusting habit. He'll soon stop that if..."

"You mean, *when* you get married?" I asked,

trying to provoke a reaction.

She sort of grunted for an answer, which didn't tell me anything.

"When *are* you getting married?" I persisted.

Mr Coletram obviously heard me say that. The dining-room window was open and he leaned in through it and said, "Next month. Isn't that right, Joan?"

Grandma Sorrell didn't say anything – just started clearing dishes away. I got up to help her, and as we loaded up the hatch through to the kitchen I tried again.

"Next month, Grandma Sorrell? Is it going to be a church wedding or a register office?"

"Not a church, certainly. I've done that once, you know." Just for a moment her face took on a soft expression. "He was a fine man, your grandfather."

"I know. I loved him, too," I said gently. Then the softness went and the shell came back.

"Mr Coletram's nice too, though," I added, to get her to talk more about him.

She made some sort of noise which I thought must have been an agreement, then there wasn't any more to be said really. So I offered to wash up, knowing that by the time I'd finished I'd definitely have to ask about the athletics meeting. I felt more determined than ever to work at the café the following day.

At that point Mr Coletram returned and before I knew it, he'd got his hands in the washing-up bowl. He was trying to be really nice all the time. I smiled to myself because that's exactly what I was doing myself. Only I'd got an ulterior motive and he hadn't... Or had he?

Grabbing a tea towel, I started to dry the dishes and Grandma Sorrell put them away.

"Grandma Sorrell?" I began carefully.

"Yes?"

"After school tomorrow there's an athletics meeting at Durley Court School. It's quite a big, important meeting and I've been chosen to run in the four hundred metres, the two hundred metres and also to do the triple jump and the relay. Isn't that great?"

I didn't like lying, but on this occasion there was no other way.

"And what time does this event finish?"

"It finishes around six and Fen's mum has offered to drop me back here afterwards, so I'd be back about six-fifteen — well, definitely by six-thirty."

She turned to me slowly and narrowed her eyes. "I do hope that this isn't a clever ploy to get to work in that café. You know that I have strictly forbidden you to go near the place all the time you're living under this roof. I don't approve of girls of your age working, anyway."

My stars! She had got it in one. It really was amazing. I'd been so careful to give just the right amount of detail. I never went red, but the others said that my eyes usually flashed when I was embarrassed or felt guilty, so I took great care to keep them on the dishes as I wiped away.

"Of course not," I replied as lightly as I could. My legs were crossed at the ankle as I said this, because it cancels out the lie if you've got some part of your body crossed.

"I'll think about it," she finally conceded.

I made a big thing of whitening my trainers and ironing my athletics skirt, to show how keen I was. Mr Coletram watched with interest. "Bet your parents are proud of you, aren't they?" he commented, pleasantly enough. I nodded and smiled but he wasn't even looking at me. His eyes were wandering round the kitchen just as they had the dining room. Perhaps he was looking forward to living permanently in such a grand house. I presumed that that was what would happen when they were married.

Just as I finished the ironing the phone rang. "That'll be Mum. Can I get it?" I called out to Grandma Sorrell as I made a lunge for the lounge.

"Go on then," she replied.

"Hello, Mum?"

"Hello, Agnès."

"Oh … hello, Dad."

I felt a sudden stab of disappointment. Never mind, I would speak to Mum afterwards.

"How are you, Agnès?"

"Fine thanks. How are you?" I asked dutifully.

"Very good. How's school?"

"Oh, you know ... same as ever. I've got an athletics meeting tomorrow, though. I've been picked for the four hundred metres, the two hundred metres, the triple jump and the relay."

"That's excellent! Well done!" he said, sounding genuinely impressed, which made me wish things would get quickly back to usual. Even Dad seemed soft compared with Grandma Sorrell. Of course, that made me feel doubly guilty for telling such a lie.

"I knew you'd be pleased that I was going to represent my school, Dad," I said very clearly, for Grandma Sorrell's benefit. She'd have to let me go, now she knew that Dad had given his seal of approval.

"Is your business trip on schedule, Dad? Or do you think you might be back earlier? Where are you now anyway?"

"We're ... in France, actually."

"I thought it was Sardinia?"

"Yes, I've already been to Sardinia. That bit's over with."

"Oh, good. When's the French bit going to be over with?"

Grandma Sorrell must have been taking in every word, but I didn't care any more, even if she did hear how desperate I was for them to come home.

"It could be sooner than we thought," he answered, which made my heart leap.

"You're not causing any problems for your grandmother, I trust?" he asked, trying to keep his voice light but sounding just a touch suspicious.

"No, course not," I answered, resisting the temptation to say, "It's the other way round, I'm afraid." I suddenly wondered if Dad knew the latest news on the marriage front. I felt a bit horrible because maybe Grandma Sorrell wanted to tell him for herself, but I decided to go for it anyway.

"Grandma Sorrell and Mr Coletram are getting married next month," I said, with the right amount of enthusiasm in my voice. "Isn't that great?"

There was an amazing pause. I knew I'd delivered the shock line of the year. I glanced over at Grandma Sorrell. She'd buried her face in a book. Then I took a quick peek at Mr Coletram. He was practically hopping from foot to foot, looking as nervous as anything. Anyone would think that Dad was Grandma Sorrell's father, and that Mr Coletram had to ask Dad's permission to marry her.

Finally Dad spoke. "Mr *who*!" Then immediately his voice changed, as though he regretted saying that, and he asked if he could have a word with Grandma Sorrell – "to congratulate her…"

That was interesting. Dad had never even heard of Mr Coletram. The plot was thickening, but I wanted to speak to Mum and I asked if that would be all right.

"Well, very quickly then … I do want to speak to your grandmother."

A moment later Mum was on the phone. "*Salut, Maman. Ça va?*"

"Yes, *bibiche*, I'm fine, thank you."

She'd answered in English but I wanted to get back to French and find out whether she was at Mami's and Papi's.

"*Où es-tu exactement en ce moment, Maman?*"

She answered in French that she was at Mami's and Papi's. This gave me a shock. I asked her why, and she answered that it was simply to visit them, that was all. Then I asked if I could speak to them, but Mum said they'd already gone to bed, which I was surprised about because they didn't usually go to bed that early.

"Are you coming back soon, Mum?" I asked in French. "I'm missing you."

She told me that she was missing me too and that they would be home as soon as they possibly could. Then I heard Dad's voice in the background reminding her that he wanted to speak to Grandma Sorrell, so Mum and I said goodbye and see you soon to each other, before I handed the phone to Grandma Sorrell.

I didn't really listen to what was being said because I was replaying the conversation I'd had with Mum. She hadn't sounded at all mysterious about the fact that she was phoning from my grandparents' house, so maybe I had been making something out of nothing. All the same, it seemed rather a long visit to me.

After a few moments I realized that what I was feeling was actually jealousy. There they were, all together – Mum, Dad, Mami, Papi and Sebastien, and here I was, out in the cold at Bleak House with Grandma Sorrell and her shifty boyfriend, or fiancé rather.

Just as I was thinking how stupid that word sounded, I heard Grandma Sorrell actually say it. I glanced at Mr Coletram and he reminded me of a big bull frog, puffing himself out proudly. He obviously liked being referred to as Grandma Sorrell's fiancé.

I hadn't been listening to much of what she had been saying to Dad, but the general tone of the conversation was that she was obviously being very firm about her decision. Again, it reminded me of a role reversal. She sounded as though she was talking to her own father. Weird!

Going over the conversation I had had with Dad about their return, I felt another little surge of optimism when I remembered that Dad had said, "It could be sooner than we thought."

I came back to earth with a thud then, because Grandma Sorrell had finished on the phone and was going on about homework. I did have quite a bit to do, but first I had to check on one thing. "Is it all right for me to go to the athletics meeting tomorrow, Grandma Sorrell?"

"Just make sure you're back by six-thirty. I don't want any repetition of today," she answered snappily, then up I went to do my homework, feeling a bit encouraged by the thought of light at the end of the tunnel, and also the fact that sooner than that, I'd be working at the café.

The one big downer as I went to sleep was the thought of Darren. I was really worried about what would happen to Mandy after I'd gone back home. And strangely enough, I was worried about Darren, too. I knew it was ridiculous to feel even a grain of pity for someone who had been so cruel to Mandy and me, but I kept picturing a little boy sitting in the corner of that shed and laboriously carving his dreadful quandary into the wood. *I am shut in.*

Chapter 8

Surprise, surprise – the following morning, Darren wasn't even on the bus. His friends were weak and pathetic without him, so Mandy and I had quite a pleasant bus ride into school for a change, and I could rest easy that she wouldn't be bothered on the way back home either.

The others couldn't believe it when I told them about what had happened after I'd left Leah's. Leah herself was back at school, better, and my tale made all five of them totally gobsmacked. Luce as usual got more involved with the story than anyone, almost as though Darren had barred *her* in a shed, and not me.

"I'll kill the big poo-bag," she announced dramatically. "I will, honestly. I'll screw his neck round till his head comes off." We all fell about laughing at that, then gradually grew serious and tried to think rationally and sensibly about what we ought to do.

"Oh, by the way," I told them happily, "I'm going to do my turn at the café after all. Grandma Sorrell bought the story about the athletics meeting. The only detail I've got to sort out is how to get home. I told her your mum was going to bring me back, Fen."

"I'm sure Mum wouldn't mind taking you back, you know," Fen immediately offered.

"Do you think she would?"

"I'll get her to pick you up at six o'clock outside the café. I'll be there too, to make sure she doesn't come right to the door with you, and spill the beans to Grandma Sorrell."

"Thanks, Fen."

"Oh – and by the way," Fen added, "I tried to find out more about Marine, the little bilingual girl, and why she won't talk, but Rachel says there's some sort of secret that nobody's supposed to know, but everyone's got to be very patient and kind, and eventually Marine's voice will come back. That's what the teachers at her school have been saying, apparently."

"She's actually lost her voice?"

"So Rachel says."

I was determined to find out more. Maybe I'd see Marine and Sylvie today.

It was great to walk in through the back door of the café to the kitchen at four o'clock. Kevin seemed pleased to see me. "How's the prisoner today?" he enquired, flippantly.

"Having two hours of freedom before I go back to my cell," I answered in the same tone.

"Good. Work hard then. You need to get your exercise. You can start with these." He was putting fatty frying pans and other cooking utensils by the sink as he spoke. I got my apron on and started to fill the sink with hot soapy water.

"Hello, pet," Jan said, flashing me a sympathetic smile. "Glad you managed to come." The others must have laid it on really thickly about what an awful time I was having at Bleak House.

"Hi, Andy," said Mark, whose turn it was. "How are you coping with the old girl then?"

I grinned at him. "Fine, thanks. Dad phoned last night and it looks as though they might be home sooner than they thought."

"Bet you can't wait."

"You're right there."

When I'd finished the washing-up I went into the café to see what I could do because Jan had mentioned that it was pretty busy in there. The first people I saw were Sylvie and Marine. I felt very flattered because their eyes lit up when they saw me.

Nobody had taken their orders, so that was a good place for me to start. Unfortunately I couldn't stay and talk because there were other customers to serve, but I did manage to say a few words in French about how my parents may be back quite soon, and then Marine and her mum could come and see us at our house.

Marine gave her usual tiny smile with its accompanying silence, but Sylvie said, "That would be great." I suddenly wondered whether everything was all right between her and her husband as she never talked about him much. Maybe something had gone badly wrong which was affecting Marine. I started trying to compose a good line about that so that when the café was a little less full, I could snatch a few minutes to chat with them.

I took two more orders and served all three. As I put Marine's banana milkshake down on the table, along with Sylvie's espresso coffee and their two little cakes, I asked Sylvie if she worked anywhere.

"No," she replied, a bit sadly I thought. "I'll go back to work one day, but – " She indicated Marine with a quick jerk of her head – "now's not such a good time. I'm needed here more than I'm needed by the old folks."

"Old folks? Did you used to work with old people then?"

"Yes, I've worked in three different old people's homes, and one day I'd like to run my own home for old people."

If you'd asked me to guess what Sylvie's job had been, I think this would have been my last guess in the world. I must have been looking at her in a curious way because she explained, "It's very calming, working with old people. They've had most of their lives, they're full of experience and wisdom and they're ready to slow down, so you're not responsible for forming them or influencing them in any way. And they always love to see you. It's a great job."

I'd listened intently to this speech because Sylvie was so sure of what she was saying. I'd never looked at old people like that before, and I thought how clever Sylvie was to see them in that light. The other reason I'd listened so carefully was because I was absolutely convinced that somewhere in that speech lay the reason why Marine was as she was. It turned out later that I was right, but at the time I couldn't make any connections.

"What's your husband's job?" I asked, hoping that this sounded like a natural follow-on to the previous conversation.

"Tom's an accountant," she answered, then smiled a fond smile. "But not one of the boring sort," she added. I immediately made a mental note to cross "husband/wife problems" off my list of why Marine wasn't talking. It was perfectly obvious, even from that brief sentence, that Sylvie adored her husband.

"Should I phone your grandmother this evening," Sylvie then asked, "to see if you can come to our place tomorrow after school?"

"Yes, that would be great," I replied warmly, as she wrote down Grandma Sorrell's phone number on the edge of a paper napkin. "But don't mention that you saw me in here, whatever you do. I'm not supposed to be here, you see. It's one of her over-the-top rules. She thinks I'm at an athletics meeting. Fen's mum is going to take me back later."

As I said that, who should walk in, but Fen and Tash. I introduced them to Sylvie, then to Marine, who didn't respond at all, then they asked me to get them Seven Ups, and went to sit down at the corner table.

"I'd better get back to work," I told Sylvie.

"Yes, of course, speak to you later then." I got the drinks for Fen and Tash, then went into the kitchen where the washing-up had piled up again. A lot of it was for the dishwasher, so I loaded it up and set it going, then plunged into the pots and pans at the sink.

Mark came over and said, "Message from Fen, 'Mrs Starebear is in the café with a man.' Great emphasis on the 'man', you notice," he added with a stupid wide-eyed look which made me laugh.

As soon as I'd finished the washing-up I went

to have a peek. I strolled in casually and made for Fen and Tash's table, glancing around subtly to try and catch a glimpse of the man. The moment I saw him I did the fastest about-turn in the world and dived back through the swing doors, because "the man" was none other than Mr Coletram!

"You look like I'd look if I'd just seen a snake," Kevin informed me.

I considered telling him what I'd just seen, but decided it was too complicated. Anyway, Kevin would't be interested. People's relationships don't grab him at all.

"I'm OK," I told him lightly, but the moment Mark came in, I got him to give a message to Fen and Tash to come into the kitchen. I busied myself with greasing flan cases and doing other jobs for Kevin while I waited.

"Mark said you wanted us," said Fen, coming in a few moments later.

"That man with Mrs Starebear – it's Leslie Coletram, Grandma Sorrell's fiancé," I told them.

Tash looked suitably surprised and intrigued but Fen just said, "So?"

"So what's he doing with another woman?" I replied.

"Having a cup of tea. What's the harm in that?" Fen replied calmly.

"Yeah, maybe I'm overreacting," I said. "It's probably just someone he's known for ages... All the same, I'd love to know what they're talking about."

"Let's listen in on their conversation," Fen said excitedly to Tash.

"It's not going to be easy from three tables away, is it?" Tash retorted sensibly.

Then, with spot-on timing, Jan flew into the kitchen and went out again almost immediately, saying, "Jaimini and Luce have just come in, by the way."

"Perfect," Fen said. "That's our excuse for changing tables. And I'm sure we can find a table for four right next to Mrs Starebear!"

"Go on, quick," I said, bundling them out through the swing door into the café.

"Can you come and help me in here, Andy?" Jan said, popping her head round the door a moment later. I'd been dreading that this would happen. She wanted me to serve table ten with their order.

"It's all there," said Kevin, indicating with a rough sweep of his hand which dishes were for table ten.

There was nothing for it. I couldn't just refuse to do it. Anyway, I reasoned with myself, it wasn't the same as seeing Grandma Sorrell herself in the café. After all, Mr Coletram wouldn't be so horrible as to tell her he'd seen me, would he? Not if I specially asked him.

I wasn't convincing myself. The only answer was to pray that he wasn't looking in my direction. In actual fact, I thought he would probably have his back to table ten, so unless Mrs Starebear drew his attention to me, I should get away without being seen.

Keeping my face turned away from Mr Coletram's table, I approached table ten with a full tray and began to dish out their food. I was careful to keep my back to their table the whole time, which made it difficult to give out some of the plates. Table ten was for six people and there were still the drinks to come.

Very often when you serve people their food, they stop talking completely, and that's exactly what happened with table ten. Because my ears were on stalks I could clearly hear Mrs Starebear's low voice.

"Looks like you've got it in the bag."

Then as I was reaching across with the last two plates of beefburgers I heard Mr Coletram's equally low voice, "It's got to be the hardest thing I've ever done, Madge. It's like trying to soften up a lump of rock."

"You keep at it, Les," came the answer. "It'll be worth it for us in the end."

"Certainly will…"

I suddenly realized I'd been frozen like a statue with the beefburgers suspended over some poor girl's place.

"Sorry," I mumbled, putting it down and turning to get back into the kitchen as quickly as possible. I would get Mark to do the drinks. It was vital now that Mr Coletram didn't see me.

I shot out at full speed, but couldn't resist casting a quick glance at his table. My blood froze. The woman must have said something, because Mr Coletram turned right round in his chair and our eyes met.

In his eyes I saw panic and horror, mingled with ... was that a touch of hate? In my eyes he must have seen sheer fright. I bolted into the cover of the kitchen and opened the big stock cupboard for no reason other than the fact that I needed a couple of minutes to calm down and think, and this was the best way to do it, staring into the stock cupboard as though sizing up what we were short of.

It gave me a jump when someone tapped me on the shoulder a moment later. It was Fen. Her eyes were reflections of my own.

"Did you hear what they said?" she asked me immediately.

"I heard him say that it was the hardest thing he'd ever done, like softening up a piece of rock. And I heard the woman telling him to keep it up because it would be worth it. And then I suddenly realized I'd stopped serving table ten their food and I missed the next bit."

"Well next, Mr Coletram said it certainly would be worth it because he'd had a look at some insurance papers the other night, and that's when he'd been locked in his own room by what he called 'that pesty girl'. Then Mrs Starebear must have caught sight of you, because before that moment you were completely hidden from her view by Mr Coletram.

"Anyway, the moment she spotted you, she hissed at him, 'Look. Is that the girl?' And he turned round and saw you. Then when he turned back she said, 'D'you think she heard us?' and he answered, 'Judging from the look she's just given me … yes.' The woman then said, 'Well, that's blown it,' and Mr Coletram put on a horrible sort of leer and said, 'Not necessarily. She's a wily one, that girl. She told her gran she was going to a sports meeting. I knew she wasn't telling the truth. So now I've got something to hold over her as blackmail.'"

I had been listening intently to every syllable Fen had spoken. "So that woman – Mrs Starebear – she's been in the café specially to look out for me, so she could report back to him? And he – Mr Coletram – he was just waiting for a chance to catch me out…"

145

"And he *has*, hasn't he?"

"Yes … but I've caught him out, too. They shouldn't have risked talking like that in the café … Mrs Starebear must have thought Tash was me. That was why she kept staring at Tash that first time…"

"I've not told you the worst bit yet, Andy…"

I felt a sick feeling in my stomach.

"The next thing, he turned to our table and said 'You lot friends with that little waitress?' and we all nodded dumbly, then he went on, 'Could one of you ask her to come here a moment … I want a word with her.'"

I did an involuntary shiver and followed Fen out into the café, because there was no point in delaying it. His eyes were on the door as I went through it. I didn't like the look in them. Neither of us smiled. He started talking as soon as I reached his side.

"You told your grandmother a big fib, didn't you, young lady?"

"Only because she wouldn't let me come and work here, and I have to. It's a commitment," I told him, making my voice stay calm. I was aware of the other four hanging on to every word I said.

"Do you know what your grandmother told me she'd do if ever she found out you'd been lying to her?"

I didn't say anything. He continued.

146

"She told me that she wouldn't hesitate to keep you locked in that bedroom."

A cold shudder of fear passed through me, but I knew I could overcome it if I tried. I imagined Grandma Sorrell saying such a thing as that to this man, and decided instantly that he was probably lying.

"That would be very stupid of her, because my father would disown her if she did that, and my grandmother loves my father more than anyone in the world," I added pointedly for his benefit.

"The fact remains, the consequences would be pretty dire for you, if ever your grandmother should discover that you had blatantly lied to her in order to do the one thing that she had expressly forbidden you to do."

He was right, so I didn't reply. Again he continued, "I gather you overheard my chat with Madge here?"

"Yes, I did. And that's something else that may well have dire consequences," I said calmly.

I heard Tash gasp when I said that, and at the same time I was aware of Mr Coletram's eyes glinting coldly, then his face took on a sly smile.

"So ... I thought you and I might have to come to some sort of arrangement as we both have our own best interests at heart. In fact, if you think about it, I could greatly improve the rest of your stay as long as you're prepared to keep quiet about what you heard today. And remember you're only a kid. You wouldn't fully understand our discussion anyway."

"Oh, I understood all right," I told him, making my voice sound positively venomous, which was how I felt about him. "You've wormed your way into Grandma Sorrell's affections so that you can get her to transfer money into your name, or something like that."

"There you are, Madge," he said, turning to the woman, "young minds don't begin to understand the complexities of the financial world. No, no, no. Your grandmother won't lose anything…"

"Then, in that case, you won't mind me reporting to her what I heard."

"As long as you don't forget to mention where it was you heard it…" he answered slyly. "And it would also be worth bearing in mind that she is, of course, much more likely to believe me than you. I mean, just coming in here has added one more lie to your collection, hasn't it?"

He'd got me. There was nothing more to be said, but I couldn't help just trying one last hit. "I presume your … ladyfriend here (I felt stupid saying that) … is going to reap the benefits of your little plan?"

"I'm his sister," the woman told me sharply. "We've worked hard all our lives and never had it easy like the likes of your grandmother who was born into riches. It's all right for some."

The sister, Madge, spoke much more roughly than her brother, and I suddenly realized that Mr Coletram's accent and way of talking was most likely all put on for Grandma Sorrell's benefit.

My mind was in a turmoil. This was a dreadful thing they were doing and yet it was none of my business. Grandma Sorrell must at least like Mr Coletram, because no one was forcing her to let him stay in her house. But I didn't like him. He had a nasty gleam in his eyes, and there may have been layers of cruelty underneath the greed, that I knew nothing about.

On the other hand, Grandma Sorrell had made my life unbearable for the last few days and could certainly make it worse if she chose. I knew without any doubt that the one thing that would make her really angry would be if she found out that I'd been working at the café.

"OK. I won't say anything," I finally said.

"That's a sensible girl," he replied in an expressionless tone. "And neither will I. Of course, you must remember that I don't like people who go back on their word, so don't even think of changing your mind, or the consequences for you will be even worse."

"Jan's closing," I heard Fen say softly, and I realized that the others were ready to go and there was no one else in the café except Mr

Coletram, his sister and me. "I'll be back with Mum at six," Fen added quietly and off she went with the others – all looking extremely subdued for once.

I held my head up and went back into the kitchen. I was in a terrible position but somehow I was determined to get out of it. For the moment, though, it was better to play along with the hateful Coletram. A tremor passed through me though, as I thought of his final threat.

Fen and I didn't speak much in front of her mum. We sat together in the back of the car, and Fen mouthed to me, "What are you going to do?" The radio was on, but all the same we didn't want Dee to hear what we were saying.

I shrugged my shoulders and gave a hopeless look in answer. Fen mouthed, "Don't do anything. We'll talk about it tomorrow." And I nodded.

The moment we got to Bleak House, I leapt out of the car, said, "Thanks very much for the lift, Dee," and hurried off round the back. I wondered whether or not Coletram would be there. I couldn't bring myself to put the "Mr" in front of his name any more. To me he was just plain Coletram from now on.

Dee was driving off as I tried the back door. It was locked. I rang the bell, and after a moment Grandma Sorrell appeared. I studied her face to find out what mood she was in. She looked her usual rather grumpy self. It suddenly occurred to me that I'd better have a few answers ready for when she asked about the athletics meeting.

"Another five minutes and I would have been worried," was her greeting.

"Don't you want to know how I got on?" I asked, trying to inject a note of happiness and pride into my voice.

"Go on then," was all she managed, and I found myself really hating her for being so uninterested in me. I followed her stiff, starchy back into the sitting room, and was tempted to tell her that I'd come last in every event, just to see if that made her at all sympathetic. I changed my mind about that, though, the moment we came into the sitting room because there, wearing a smile that didn't reach his eyes, sat callous Coletram. I was dreading having to lie in front of him. Although I knew I wouldn't be blushing, I felt sure my guilt must have showed.

"I came second in the relay and the triple jump, and won the two hundred metres *and* the four hundred metres."

It was horrible delivering these lines, because I was weakening my position even more. The more I lied to Grandma Sorrell, especially in front of Coletram, the more I had to lose, if ever she found me out.

"And where's your kitbag?"

"I left it at school."

"Doesn't your kit need washing after all that?"

"I've got PE again tomorrow, so I thought I'd wash it tomorrow night."

"We'll be eating in half an hour. Go and get on with your homework now, until I call you."

I turned to go and thought how cruel she was not even congratulating me on my success. Then I remembered that of course it was all made up anyway. As my hand turned the door knob to go out of the sitting room, she suddenly said, "Well done, Agnès. For a little girl, you're certainly a very fast runner."

Those few words made everything different in my mind. It had been better before she had spoken, because now I felt horribly guilty about deceiving her, and I also knew that I had to warn her about Coletram's evil intentions. Grandma Sorrell wasn't really cruel. She was just so sharp-tongued, strict and unused to children that she came over as cruel. Next to Coletram she was about as cruel as Cinderella!

"Yes, well done, Andy," he suddenly said with just enough sarcasm in his voice for *me* to detect, without Grandma Sorrell noticing. I kept my head turned away from them so no one would notice my eyes flashing.

It was later, while we were eating our baked

potatoes, that the phone rang. I prayed it might be Mum. I was going to gabble out as much as I could in French – anything to make her come home quickly. Even if it wasn't Mum I'd planned to phone her later, if necessary in the middle of the night. It would be terrible if she wasn't at Mami and Papi's, but there was nothing for it. Mami and Papi would understand that I had to disturb them. They would listen to my incredible story and tell me what I ought to do.

It wasn't Mum. It was Sylvie phoning to ask if I could go to her house after school the next day. Grandma Sorrell repeated her name. That's how I knew it was her, then she said "I see" a lot and finally stated, rather rudely I thought, that I'd have to be back by six at the latest.

"Can I speak to her?" I interrupted in a loud whisper, so Grandma Sorrell handed the phone to me. "Hi, Sylvie."

"Hi, Andy. Phew! I see what you mean about your grandmother," she said, lowering her voice slightly.

"That's right," I said in my most normal voice as though Sylvie had commented on how warm it was for the time of year, or something.

"If you walk down to the café after school, I'll meet you there, and we can go on to my place after that," Sylvie was saying. "And I'll run you back for six o'clock. Don't worry."

"OK. Thanks very much Sylvie, see you tomorrow."

"Bye Andy, see you."

Good. That was something nice to look forward to. After I put the phone down Coletram spoke.

"I'm glad you said six o'clock, Joan, because I have an invitation for you. I'd like to take you and Andy out to a favourite pub of mine tomorrow evening for a nice meal to celebrate our good news."

Was this another slimy gesture of his to get even further into her affections, or what? The thought of an evening out was like a breath of fresh air, but I couldn't think of two people I'd less like to spend it with.

Grandma Sorrell had the appearance of someone who'd like to look pleased but didn't know how to, so the expression that came out was a peculiar grimace. "Well, I'm sure we'll enjoy that, won't we, Agnès?"

I gritted my teeth. "Yes, I'm sure we will."

Coletram's face leered at me across the table, and I shivered at the memory of his threatening words…

"…*don't even think of changing your mind, or the consequences for you will be even worse.*"

Chapter 9

At school the next day I filled the others in on what had happened since the café. I told them about the phone call from Sylvie, the proposed outing to the pub with Coletram and Grandma Sorrell, and the fact that when I'd tried to ring my French grandparents' house at two o'clock in the morning, having set my alarm for that time, there was no reply.

"They obviously just sleep very deeply," Leah said reasonably.

"But Mum can't have been there because she answered immediately the last time I phoned."

"Your mum did say that she was just visiting them though, didn't she?" Tash pointed out. "She's obviously gone on somewhere else with your father where it must have been quite difficult to phone from."

"Anyone can phone from anywhere if they

really want to," I insisted, knowing that I sounded rather babyish but recalling the loneliness I had felt hearing all those rings of the phone down in the south of France.

Tash obviously felt really sorry for me and so did Leah. They each put an arm round me, and Leah suggested that perhaps my parents were going to surprise me and turn up unexpectedly.

I nodded and tried to get free from their protective arms without making it too obvious. I don't like people feeling all that sorry for me.

"Guess who came on the bus and didn't say a single word this morning?" I asked suddenly, which made Tash and Leah drop their arms.

"Darren Kirk," Luce replied, leaning forwards ready for an interesting bit of gossip.

"I felt quite sorry for him actually," I went on.

"You *what*!" Fen almost exploded. "You're getting like Leah, Andy. Just think of what he did to you and Mandy. Surely you can't feel sorry for him after that?"

"But what made you feel sorry in the first place?" Leah wanted to know.

"He had a black eye and a swollen lip."

"His own stupid fault for fighting," Jaimini said, quite aggressively for her. The others all nodded in agreement.

"Nobody would fight Darren and come off better than him," I pointed out.

"So what are you saying?"

"I think his dad did it. Apparently Darren's mum works at the same pub where Mandy's mum, Lara, works. Only Darren's mum works in the kitchen. Lara once told Mandy that she felt sorry for Darren's mum because she must lead a tough life being married to a brute like Darren's father."

"That explains why Lara didn't really say much when she found out it was Darren who had shut Mandy in the shed. Mandy told me that Lara said Darren would be punished enough by his father. Then sure enough, Darren turns up this morning looking like that. He must have looked even worse yesterday. That's probably why he didn't come to school."

"That doesn't make it any fairer on you and Mandy when he's so horrible, though," Fen pointed out.

"I'm not sure he will be horrible any more," I told them.

They were looking puzzled, so I went on. "You see, as soon as Mandy filled me in on Darren's family this morning, I felt sorry for him. Then one of the older boys, who gets on at a later stop, started making comments to Darren like, 'Ugh, who's made you look even uglier than usual, then?' So I went up to the back of the bus and said, 'Well, it obviously wasn't you. You wouldn't

157

dare raise a finger against him, would you? But you think you're ever so brave with words, don't you?' "

"Andy! You said that with all those year-ten boys around, including Darren?" Leah asked, amazed.

"And what did he say?" the others chorused.

"Nothing, absolutely nothing. They all started looking out of the windows, so I went back to my place, but as I was getting off the bus, Darren passed me, and without looking at me, he mumbled 'Cheers'."

"You're so brilliant, Andy," Leah said warmly, and all the others were congratulating me and giving me compliments till I felt my cheeks burning, even if it didn't show.

"Anyway, what am I going to do about Coletram?" I asked.

"Don't do anything," Fen said promptly. "Go to the restaurant and act completely normally. But keep your ears and eyes open. Look for clues that may help you decide what's best to do. That's my advice."

"Yes, that's my advice too," Luce agreed, looking proudly around, as though she and not Fen had said it all, which made everybody laugh.

After school it was Jaimini's turn to work at the café. I waved to her through the window as I went off happily with Marine and Sylvie.

It was a flat where the three of them lived together. It was fairly small but Sylvie had made it look lovely with plants and mirrors, and rugs on the walls, soft squashy chairs with old-fashioned flowery covers, old pine furniture and little ornaments like candlesticks, and bowls of pot pourri everywhere.

Jaimini would absolutely love this place, I thought. Sylvie chatted away from the kitchen as she made me a drink with her soda stream. The door was open between the kitchen and the sitting room so it was easy to hear her. Marine sat quietly on a big cushion in the sitting room, cuddling a soft toy rabbit and watching me looking at all the photos everywhere.

There were loads of pictures of a little boy. At least, I presume it was a boy. He was scarcely more than a baby – about the same age as Sebastien, I guessed.

"Who's this, Marine?" I asked her, taking one of the pictures of the baby boy over to show her. I crouched down beside her and smiled encouragingly at the still little figure on the cushion. Then I jumped up as though she'd bitten me, because without warning, she burst into floods and floods of loud, sobbing tears, burying her face in the cushion, and thumping it hard at the same time.

Sylvie didn't say a word, just ran in from the kitchen, scooped up Marine and held her tightly while stroking her hair, rocking her and murmuring, "It's all right, darling, it's all right." Then she looked up at me and said, "Don't worry, Andy… She'll be OK in a few minutes."

"But what…?" I began, feeling shaky and bewildered.

"Marine had a little brother called Christopher, who died last year. It was a cot death. She hasn't spoken since. After six months without a word from her, and no sign of her getting over Christopher's death, we decided to move so that she could have a fresh start at a new school. That's why we came here."

"I'm really sorry," I said, sitting down before my legs collapsed.

"We've tried everything we can, to help her get over it," Sylvie went on. "I'm so sorry you had to find out like this," she added. "I was going to tell you the moment I got the chance."

I nodded and felt really guilty that I'd been so insensitive and thoughtless. It was suddenly clear to me why Sylvie had said how much she liked looking after old people, because you didn't have to feel responsible for them. Poor Sylvie. Poor Marine.

After a bit, Marine's sobs subsided and then she raised her head, but she'd gone into a big decline and wouldn't play with any of the toys I kept offering her.

A little later Tom came home. He was a really nice man and I felt ever so sorry for this little family that would have been so happy, if such an awful tragedy hadn't happened to them.

Tom tried the light-hearted approach with Marine, tickling her and trying to make her laugh using funny voices with her glove puppets. He raised a smile or two from her and said, "That's better."

Shortly afterwards I said I ought to go, and Tom offered to take me back. In the car I told him about Sebastien and asked him whether he thought Marine would react badly to another little boy. Tom shrugged. "Who knows?" he answered. "It might make her better. Then again it might make her worse, but I reckon it's worth a try. Anything's worth a try."

At six-thirty on the dot we were all ready to go off to the pub. Mrs Hatch, the nosey neighbour, passed the drive with her dog. "Off out?" she asked conversationally.

"Yes, we're going to the Woodcock. They do very good food there," Grandma Sorrell replied. "You ought to try it one day."

"I'm not a great one for going out," replied Mrs Hatch. "Apart from taking Tessa for her walk," she added. "I hope you all have a lovely evening." It crossed my mind that this must have been one of the longest conversations Grandma Sorrell had ever had with Mrs Hatch. It wasn't until later that evening that I attached any importance to this fact.

Grandma Sorrell belted up and switched on the ignition. She was wearing a nasty pale blue outfit for the occasion, and Coletram wore the most skanky brown suit you've ever seen. I'd changed into jeans and a sweatshirt.

We must have looked a strange trio as we went into the Woodcock. It was a very big pub with the bar at one end and the restaurant at the other. Coletram led us into the restaurant.

"Hi, Andy," came a voice from behind me and I turned to see Lara pulling a pint of beer behind the bar. So this was where she worked.

"Hello, Lara," I called back, then rolled my eyes to show her I was only here with Grandma Sorrell and Coletram under sufferance. She grinned back at me. The kitchen door opened as we were walking past and I looked in.

I could see a small, thin woman vigorously wiping surfaces. Her face was ugly, there was no other word for it. And it was made worse by one of those purplish birthmarks called wine stains, on her cheek, which went right down her neck as well. Lara came up to show us to our table, and as she went past me, seeing me look in the kitchen, she whispered, "That's Darren's mum." No wonder Darren went on about Mandy's perfect mum. It was obviously just a defence mechanism because of his own mum.

"Here we are, Mr Coletram," Lara was saying with her best hostess smile, as we sat down at the table she had indicated. She handed us each a menu and went back to the bar as the manager appeared.

"Good evening, Mr Coletram. How are you?" he said.

"I'm very well, thank you," Coletram replied. "May I introduce you to Joan Sorrell, my wife-to-be, and her granddaughter, Agnès."

The manager said he was very pleased to meet us, and shook Grandma Sorrell's hand, murmuring his congratulations about the forthcoming happy event. He smiled vaguely at me, then the three of them got engrossed in a conversation about what fish was on the menu, and as nobody was taking any notice of me I murmured that I was going to the loo then nipped off to have a word with Lara. I stopped half-way to the bar because it was obvious she was busy serving customers.

I had actually stopped right next to the open kitchen door, and once again, could see in. Darren's mum saw me looking and asked if I wanted anything. She sounded really kind and gave me a small, embarrassed smile. I noticed she tried to turn her face so that I wouldn't see her birthmark.

Giving her a big beam, I said, "I just thought I'd say hello. My name's Andy, and I know Lara and Mandy and Darren." The moment I'd said Darren's name her face seemed to sort of crumple into a mass of worried lines, and her hands, still holding the cloth, wound it round and round. I felt so sorry for her; with a brute of a husband, and a son like Darren, she must lead the most awful life. I was racking my brains to think what to say next, but I needn't have bothered because she had turned to the sink and was engrossed in washing up, so I went on to the bar, where Lara was free.

"You're early, aren't you?" she said immediately. "And where's his sister? I thought she was coming too." I must have looked puzzled because she went on, "That … what's 'er name? Madge, that's it. I'm sure I heard them in here yesterday lunchtime arranging it for seven o'clock tonight. He was giving her directions to your grandmother's place."

As Lara was telling me this I felt my heart thudding. Suddenly I knew exactly what was going on. Coletram had cunningly contrived it so that Bleak House would be empty, which meant that Madge could go in there and … and what? And burgle the place, perhaps. Maybe she would help herself to Grandma Sorrell's jewellery or her credit cards or something. Coletram must have told Madge where the spare key is kept, or maybe he'd had one cut from his own key.

Then an even worse thought occurred to me. Maybe he was planning on blaming the missing items on me. I had to think quickly. My watch said ten to seven. If I went back and told Grandma Sorrell my hunch, she'd think me totally mad, and tell me to stop talking nonsense.

Even if it turned out that I was right, it would be impossible to prove who had done it unless we caught Madge in the act. I didn't want Coletram to have any inkling at all that it was me who had put Grandma Sorrell on to it. No, I somehow needed to get her back to Bleak House to find out for herself.

My brain was ticking over at a hundred miles per hour and I suddenly remembered that nosey neighbour, Mrs Hatch. A plan was forming in my mind but I needed to act fast.

"Lara," I hissed, because she was putting money in the till. I glanced over to the restaurant and our table wasn't in view from where I was standing. Lara came over to me and I spoke to her in a rapid whisper.

"I can't go into any explanations now, but I'm

almost certain that my grandma's going to be burgled tonight. That Mr Coletram's up to no good."

Lara was frowning at me as though she thought I had an overactive imagination.

"You've got to believe me, Lara. I've caught him in the middle of the night rifling through her papers and I've overheard him talking to Madge." Lara's eyes widened. "Can you lend me twenty pence for the phone and then when it rings in about five minutes, can you make sure you answer it?"

She gave me twenty pence from behind the bar, but still wore her frown as she said, "I only hope you're right about all this."

I punched in Luce's number on the phone by the bar, and prayed she'd answer it herself. My prayer was answered. "Luce, it's Andy," I said softly. "Listen carefully. Have you got a pen?"

"Yes," she answered, obviously shocked into wasting not a moment by the serious sound of my voice.

"Write down this number." I gave her the pub's number. "In five minutes precisely, can you phone that number and ask to speak to Mrs Sorrell. You've got to pretend to be her nosey neighbour, called Mrs Hatch, and tell her you're sorry to interrupt her nice evening at the pub, but you think she may have an intruder, because you were just coming back from walking your dog, Tessa, when you noticed a woman in Grandma Sorrell's drive, bending down by the corner of the house, and then going round the side, looking rather furtive. Have you got all that?"

"Where was she bending down?"

"At the *corner* of the house – that's where she keeps the spare key, you see – then going round the *side*, OK?"

"Yeah, I've got it."

"Do me the voice," I ordered Luce.

She said a few words in a rather flat voice.

"Yeah, that's brilliant," I encouraged her. "Just a big higher." After a few more tries she sounded pretty convincing, which is amazing when you remember that she'd never even met the woman. "You're a genius, Luce. I'll explain everything later. Good luck."

"I hope I don't let you down."

"You won't. Bye."

I put the phone down and hurried back to my place thinking how fortunate it was that Luce was such a skilful actress. You could rely on her to impersonate anyone. I only prayed that Grandma Sorrell would take the bait.

"You've been a long time," she said as I sat down.

"I had to wait in a queue," I replied, hoping there weren't five or six loos in the place.

"I've ordered your food."

"What about a drink, Andy?" Coletram said.

"Lemonade, please," I told him, trying to act as normally as possible, then I began to talk about poor little Marine, because I thought it was better than sitting tensely waiting for the phone. I heard it ring but didn't react at all, and a moment later Lara appeared at our table.

"Excuse me, Mrs Sorrell, there's a phone call for you," she said quietly.

Grandma Sorrell's eyebrows knitted together, but she got up and followed Lara back to the phone.

"Did she give Mum and Dad this number?" I asked Coletram as innocently as possible, so he wouldn't suspect me of anything.

He didn't even answer me. His eyes were darting about nervously and I noticed he kept swallowing. In no time at all Grandma Sorrell was back at the table.

"It's that neighbour of mine, Mrs Hatch. She's had a fall. Silly old thing. She was most apologetic about disturbing me, but there's only the one other house round there, and apparently they're away."

Grandma Sorrell had taken the car keys from her bag during this. "Get them to hold the food back, Leslie, I'll be back in fifteen minutes. Agnès, you'd better come with me. I might need a spot of help."

With those imperious words and me in her wake, she sailed out of the pub, leaving Coletram swallowing hard and looking more uncomfortable than I'd ever seen him.

Clever old Grandma Sorrell to think of that story. But why hadn't she simply told him the truth? Did she already suspect him or something? I decided to keep quiet unless spoken to. The journey to Bleak House was therefore a totally silent one with Grandma Sorrell driving fast and leaning forward over the wheel with her mouth set in a thin grim line.

Just before she turned into the drive she said briefly, "Apparently, we may have an intruder. I didn't want to mention it to … er…" She, too, seemed unable to say his name.

"…Mr Coletram," I helped her out. I got a curt nod in return.

I'd never seen Grandma Sorrell move so fast as she did at that moment. She was out of that car and into the house before you could say Whodunnit.

She hitched up her skirt and took the stairs two at a time with me just behind her, then she stood still as a statue staring into her bedroom. I stood at her side and gasped. I'd never seen her bedroom before. It was heavily decorated with thick red and gold wallpaper and deep mustard-coloured velvet curtains down to the floor. There was a huge four-poster bed with mustard drapes around it and a red and gold bedspread. The carpet was very pale green and the dressing table had three tilting mirrors and a pale green curtain round the legs. The wardrobe was the same dark mahogany, and there were two chests of drawers, also dark and gleaming.

In front of the dressing table, reflected from all sides in the tilting mirrors, standing as if transfixed, was Madge, holding two fistfuls of jewellery.

Her jaw dropped and her face went white when she saw us standing there. Then as if in slow motion her hands uncurled and the glittering jewellery slid to the floor and scattered around the carpet, glinting up at us.

"Phone the police, Agnès," Grandma Sorrell commanded me in her coldest voice. I was dashing off downstairs when she called me back. "There's a phone in here." So we both went inside the bedroom and she closed the door, standing with her back against it as I dialled 999 and gave Grandma Sorrell's name and address, explaining that we had caught a female intruder.

All through this Madge stood still and silent, looking daggers at me, while Grandma Sorrell looked daggers at her.

"So … you must be Madge," Grandma Sorrell suddenly said as I was replacing the phone. I gasped because this showed that I was right. She had suspected something.

"Very good work, Agnès," she went on, still without taking her eyes off Madge. "Your friend's imitation of Mrs Hatch was pretty good – you must remember to congratulate her. The only reason I knew it wasn't the real Mrs Hatch was because I'd arranged for Mrs Hatch to phone me herself at the Woodcock and say she'd had a fall."

I was completely shocked by what Grandma Sorrell was saying, although one thing had slid into place in my mind. I now understood why she had appeared so unusually friendly with Mrs Hatch earlier on. This was all for Coletram's benefit – to prepare the scene for Mrs Hatch's phone call. Everything else was a mystery to me, though.

"But how did you know about the burglary?" I asked her in bewilderment.

"Tell you later," she said, and then the most amazing thing happened. She shot me a quick smile and chuckled wickedly to herself.

A few minutes later we heard a noise downstairs and Grandma Sorrell said, "That'll be the police. Go down and tell them we're up here, Agnès."

I went skipping down the stairs and straight into the arms of Coletram – literally. He grabbed me, held me tight with one arm and slapped his other hand over my mouth. "Where's your grandmother?" he hissed in my ear, releasing his hand the tiniest bit for me to reply.

"Upstairs."

The hand clamped back on to my mouth, and he marched me upstairs.

As we approached the bedroom I made as much noise as I could to warn Grandma Sorrell that I was in trouble. She must have heard something because the bedroom door opened as we got up to it. Coletram shoved me through it, then closed it behind us and locked us all in. He also turned the light off, before roughly grabbing hold of me and clamping his hand over my mouth again. Although it wasn't completely dark it was very hard to see.

"The police are on their way," Madge told him immediately.

"Who called them?"

"She did." Madge pointed to me. Grandma Sorrell's triumphant expression had gone, and in its place was a frown. I knew that like mine, her brain would be doing overtime trying to think how to alert the police.

"I shouldn't make a sound, if you don't want the girl to get hurt," Coletram said ominously to Grandma Sorrell. Then he gave us one of his horrible leering smiles. "There are no lights on downstairs. The police will knock at the door, get

172

no reply, presume that the girl got it wrong and go away."

"That's a pretty naïve view," Grandma Sorrell said scornfully. "If they get no reply, they'll be all the more suspicious, won't they? You're a fool, Coletram. I knew I couldn't trust you, but I never thought you'd go to these lengths to get your hands on my money."

"I wouldn't have had any trouble at all if that granddaughter of yours hadn't turned up," he said, raising his voice but only slightly. At that moment I could have sworn I heard a noise downstairs. I knew I had to act fast. With all my strength I jolted myself out of Coletram's grip, whacking him in the stomach in the process, then I stamped hard on his foot and began pummelling the bedroom door while yelling at the top of my voice, "We're up here. He's locked us in."

All this happened in just a few seconds. To my horror I realized that Coletram was making another grab for me. I dived out of the way but Grandma Sorrell carried on what I had started by banging him on the head with a book. It threw him off balance and gave him a shock, which gave *us* another precious second or two to shout loudly. And all through this Madge just stood there looking stupid.

"Do something!" Coletram hissed at her, but it was too late. The door was flung open, having been forced by two policemen. They took in the situation at a glance and slapped handcuffs on Coletram. "That's his accomplice," Grandma Sorrell said pointing to Madge, then as we turned away, leaving the rest to the police, her arm went round me.

We went downstairs like that. Her old hand laying trembling on my shoulder, and as we walked I tried to decide whether she was supporting me, or whether it was actually the other way round.

Chapter 10

On the bus the following morning – Thursday – I told Mandy about the great adventure. She was a fantastic audience, hanging on to my every word.

Without saying anything, Darren had sat only a few places behind me. His mates, who must have been rather startled by this, automatically sat near him.

Half-way through my tale I turned round and said conversationally, "Saw your mum last night, Darren. She's really nice."

The looks on Darren's friends' faces were amazing. You would have thought I'd said, "I saw your mum last night, Darren, and she turned into a polar bear before my very eyes, but I gather she does that every night."

They turned their open-mouthed faces on Darren as if to say, "Come on, let's hear you answer that lippy little year eight."

"Yeah, she said she'd seen you," said Darren. I can't exactly say he sounded friendly, but it was such an improvement on his normal way of talking to me that nobody on the bus could believe our little exchange. Just about everybody had stopped talking to listen to the strange phenomenon of Darren Kirk talking to a year-eight girl.

"Was that the police at your grandmother's place?" he went on.

I nodded. "We had an intruder."

"Yeah?" said a year-ten girl, looking impressed.

"Two intruders actually, but they didn't get away with anything."

"Weren't you scared?" one of the year-nine girls asked, because I had the attention of the whole bus by then.

After that everyone asked me tons of questions about the intruders but I held back on the details because of not wanting Grandma Sorrell to look a fool in their eyes. Also, I wanted my close friends to be the first to hear the full story. Darren didn't say anything else but his mates did. They were really wrapped up in the drama, and they obviously thought it was OK to talk to me now that their great leader had done so. They're such sheep, these boys.

It was Mrs Payne driving the bus that day, and as we piled off at school, she took my arm and held me back till the very end. I wondered what on earth she wanted to say to me. When there was no one apart from the two of us left on the bus, she said, "I've been driving school buses for years now and I reckon I'd make a pretty good child psychologist, I know that much about kids' behaviour. But what you've done on this bus beats anything I've ever seen. You've got those big louts in your pocket, and you've pulled the whole bus together, and for that you deserve a medal."

Her stern face broke into a fond smile and I knew I'd always remember that moment. I felt so proud as I skipped off down the steps and ran into school.

At break time I told my burglary story in depth, with the others pressing me to go over bits of it in even more detail. I came in for lots of praise and felt really happy, but the best moment of all came when a prefect appeared on the netball courts and said, "Is Andy Sorrell here?"

"Yes," I answered.

"Phone message from your mum." She handed me a small piece of yellow paper from the school secretary. It said: *Your mother phoned. Parents are back. Please go straight home after school.*

When I'd scanned the paper I handed it to Leah, then one by one all the others quickly read it. I think the prefect must have thought us totally mad because we all punched the air and screeched, "Yessssssss!"

I could hardly wait till the end of school I was so desperate to see Mum and Dad and Sebastien again. Leah went off to the café because it was her turn to work as she'd swapped with Tash, and I ran all the way home and burst into the house.

Mum came rushing out of the kitchen with her arms flung wide to hug me. Dad followed just behind her and joined in on the edge of the hug. Sebastien toddled behind and fought his way into the middle of us.

"He can walk all on his own!" I exclaimed. Then I let go of them all suddenly, because over Mum's shoulder I could see Mami and Papi coming slowly towards us. They looked somehow older and frailer than usual but with the same lovely smiles. I could have cried with happiness. I gave them both lots of hugs and kisses and said, "So that's why there was no reply when I phoned your house in the middle of the night on Tuesday!"

"We wanted to surprise you," said Mum.

"But we had to break the journey in two, and stayed overnight last night in northern France," Dad explained as we all went back into the kitchen. There I got another surprise, because Grandma Sorrell was sitting in the armchair in the corner.

"We've just been hearing all about your incredible adventures," Mum said.

Grandma Sorrell and I gave each other a conspiratorial look, and I saw Dad smile.

"Andeeee," Sebastien said, banging on my leg with his little fist. I picked him up and for once he stayed snuggled in my shoulder, without wriggling, as if he knew this was a very special homecoming.

After that we talked and talked for ages. It turned out that Mum hadn't been on a business trip with Dad at all. She'd been looking after Mami and Papi who'd been really ill with legionnaires' disease. Mum had been terrified they were going to die, though she didn't tell me that till later when we were on our own.

"But why didn't you tell me where you were really going?" I asked Mum.

"Because you would have either inseested on coming too, wheech wouldn't have worked because of school, or uzzerwise you'd have worried yourself seek. I deedn't know how long I was going to be needed. It was all such a shock when they were both so eel at the same time."

"And how long are you staying with us in England?" I asked Mami and Papi.

"*Toujours*," replied Papi, with a twinkle in his eye.

"For ever?" I asked incredulously.

"I'm not reesking leaving them alone again," Mum explained. "From now on, they are going to

179

leeve with us where I can keep an eye on them. We've got thees enormous house where we all rattle around. Eet'll be lovely to have eet filled a bit more. I only weesh we knew some more old people who understand French…"

"I might just be able to help you there," I told Mum secretively. "Not old, but … perfect!"

I glanced at Grandma Sorrell in the corner. She would never be one of us. She was different, much more independent – a loner. All the same I couldn't help feeling a small pang of pity for her, going back to Bleak House with not even a second marriage to look forward to.

"Don't you worry about me, Andy," she said, calling me by my nickname for the first time ever, and obviously catching my look of sympathy. "I'm fond of my own company – always have been and always will be. It's a positive relief to have that man out of my life."

"But tell me, Grandma Sorrell…"

"Oh, let's dispense with Grandma Sorrell, shall we? It's such a mouthful. Just say Gran or whatever you prefer."

"But tell me, *Gran*," I said pointedly, which made Mum and Dad laugh, "when did you first realize that Mr Coletram was not all he seemed?"

"Well, I first suspected him before you even appeared on the scene. I was just biding my time, because I was fairly sure I'd catch him out, if he was up to any mischief. But you know, in a funny way I didn't want to find him out, because I wanted to believe that it really was me he cared about and not my money. He thought he could get me to transfer my money bit by bit into his name once we were married. Then I suppose he planned to divorce me or just make off with the money, I don't know. Unfortunately for him, you appeared on the scene, and that put a spoke in the wheel. He and his sister thought they'd better move fast so they set up the burglary…"

Grandma Sorrell looked suddenly tired. "I know I'm a bad-tempered old thing, but there's nothing more guaranteed to make me mad than the thought that I'm losing my grip on things. And somehow, with you and all your energy around, Andy, that's how I felt."

Now we'd started talking about it all, I couldn't stop. After the police had finally left the previous evening, Grandma Sorrell had looked pretty exhausted and I could tell she didn't want to talk. I had made us both toast and hot chocolate, then Grandma Sorrell had gone straight to bed while I watched some television before going to bed.

"But yesterday evening, did you suspect what Coletram had got planned, even before Luce phoned you?"

"In the back of my mind, yes. He appeared to be totally ill at ease, and I also got the impression he was wary of you. So when the phone call came, I put two and two together, and realized you were one step ahead of him. I was proud of you at that moment, you know…" Grandma Sorrell gave my hand an embarrassed pat as she said that, and I noticed she'd got little tears at the corners of her eyes. She was human, after all!

There was a pause, then Dad said, "Come on, you'll have plenty of time for talking, but now, let's celebrate." He picked up the phone. "What's the number of that café, Agnès?"

I told him and he tapped it in. When he'd spoken to Jan and she'd agreed to keep the café open after closing time, he told me to get on to all my friends so they could come along and join in the celebrations too. I phoned Luce, who phoned Jaimini, then Fen, who phoned Tash.

"There's one more phone call I'd like to make, Dad."

"Go ahead," Dad said. His sudden good spirits were quite a shock to the system I can tell you … but a pleasant one! Everyone was talking when I made the last phone call so nobody heard me.

About half an hour later we piled into two cars and off we went. I saw Dad put various bottles in the boot, and also some nice-looking French bread and cheese, and blocks of chocolate.

We got there before the others, so Leah and I set everything up, putting four tables together in the middle with all the food and drink and plates and glasses on them. Then we pulled the rest of the tables to the sides of the café, and just put the chairs in a semicircle so people like Mami and Papi could sit down.

Sebastien, in a pair of red dungarees, was tottering round and round all the chairs, holding on to them and shouting happily. Jan, who loves babies and toddlers, bent down and played "peepo" with him which made him giggle and say something like "car" which I knew meant "encore", the French for "again". After a bit I think Jan regretted having started the game in the first place.

Mami and Papi sat smiling in the middle of our semicircle of chairs. They must have really been enjoying their first taste of England. It was going to be lovely to have them living in our house.

After a bit, Luce, Jaimini, Fen and Tash all came and I introduced them to Mami and Papi and Grandma Sorrell. (It was going to take me a while to get used to saying Gran!) Then Dad picked up a bottle of champagne and said, "Right, is everybody here?"

"No, Dad, my special guests haven't arrived yet."

And as I spoke the door opened and in came Sylvie, Tom and Marine. I went over to welcome them, then introduced them to everyone they didn't know. Marine as usual followed silently in her parents' wake, and only managed the tiniest smile for me. Sylvie explained to Mami and Papi that Marine was bilingual and very shy, then she chatted away with them in French and I could tell that Mami and Papi really liked her and would be seeing a lot of her.

Then quite suddenly, from behind the counter where he had been hidden, appeared Sebastien. He stood there on his little wobbly legs with a big grin on his face and called out "Car" to Jan.

And that's when the miracle happened. Dad popped the champagne cork just as Marine's little voice rang out, "*Comment s'appelle-t-il, ton petit frère, Andy?*"

I could scarcely answer her I was so shocked. "He's called Sebastien," I managed to reply.

"*Sebastien? Il est mignon,*" she said with a wide smile. That means "He's sweet." Then she went over to him and handed him her rabbit which he pretended to kiss. "*Tu aimes bien le petit lapin?*" she asked, before turning to Sylvie. "Look Mum, he likes my little rabbit. Look."

And at the sound of her daughter's voice, after all this time, the tears in Sylvie's eyes spilled over on to her cheeks. All my friends looked pretty choked, too. Tom's arm went round Sylvie and he gave me a big thumbs-up sign. The other adults didn't really know why we were all so moved, except Grandma Sorrell, whose glass was the last to be filled with the bubbling champagne that Dad was pouring out and Jan was handing round.

"Raise your glasses," she commanded imperiously. We all obeyed her, naturally. "Here's to Marine, Sebastien and the rabbit," she said, which made Luce laugh out loud.

"You can't toast a rabbit, Grandma Sorrell!"

I didn't think Grandma Sorrell had ever been called that by anyone but me, but she must have liked it, because she turned to Luce, actually grinned(!) and said, "You certainly can, young lady. And incidentally, that was an excellent imitation of my neighbour that you did the other evening!" Luce thanked her, then blow me, Grandma Sorrell took another big swig of champagne and held her glass up again. Everyone followed suit.

"And here's to my granddaughter Andy, who one day will be a very famous detective or spy or something. And when that day comes people will turn to one another and say, 'Wherever did she get this extraordinary talent from?' And you know what the answer will be, don't you? Hm…?"

Grandma Sorrell's eyes travelled round the little group of smiling, waiting faces. "It will be … her grandmother! And you know why, don't you, Andy?" I shook my head, wondering what on earth she was going to say, and into the brief silence came Dad's voice whispering to Mum so only I could hear.

"Had the old bird been drinking before she came here or something?" Mum gave Dad a friendly whack on the knee, then Grandma Sorrell gave me the answer to her own question.

"Because her grandmother isn't such an old fool that she thinks her granddaughter talks to her gorilla in the middle of the night, and says her history project out loud. Nor is she too silly and doddery to put two and two together when she finds a long blonde hair in the bedroom the next day!"

With that her eyes rested on Leah, who blushed, then burst out laughing because Grandma Sorrell was chuckling away. I'll never forget that moment – it reminded me of dominoes tumbling into each other as one by one everyone joined in the laughter. The last person to join in was Marine, but I think hers was the happiest laughter I'd ever heard, as though she'd woken up from a bad dream.

"To Andy," repeated Grandma Sorrell, her twinkling eyes resting on me.

"To Andy," came the answering cry, and I hugged the precious moment to myself and looked down, thinking that that must be the loner in me – the part of me that takes after Grandma Sorrell.

Join

Would you and your friends like to know more
about Fen, Tash, Leah, Andy, Jaimini and Luce?

We have produced a special bookmark to
commemorate the launch of the Café Club
series. To get yours free, together with a
special newsletter about Fen and her friends,
their creator, author Ann Bryant, and advance
information about what's coming next in
the series, write (enclosing a self-addressed
label, please) to:

The Café Club
c/o the Publicity Department
Scholastic Children's Books
Commonwealth House
1-19 New Oxford Street
London WC1A 1NU

We look forward to hearing from you!